I0755864

Sex, drugs, and rock and roll in the Andes—this account of a road trip by three young American men captures the spirit of the 70's and describes a world on the verge of change. Traveling from California these innocents abroad drug, whore, smuggle, and rock their way to Buenos Aires and back on a six-month, 12,400 mile overland odyssey that recalls the *Motorcycle Diaries* and *On the Road*. Told in both travelogue and fiction, this two-books-in-one describes the great cultural gulf between the United States and Latin America at a time when native population are excluded from modern society and ruthless generals kill the youth who oppose them. Seemingly oblivious to the dangers that constantly stalk them, three hippies manage to find a time of pure freedom in South America.

Hippies in the Andes

by
jeffrey marcus oshins

Deep Six Publishers
Johnson & Associates
PO Box 4072
Santa Barbara, CA 93140
805-683-1200
www.deepsixpub.com

Printed in the United States of America.

ISBN Paperback: 978-0-9831981-5-4
ISBN Hardback: 978-8987787-1-4
ISBN ebook: 978-0-9831981-4-7

Library of Congress Control Number: 2013944343

Publisher's Cataloguing-in-Publication Data

Oshins, Jeffrey Marcus, 1950-

Hippies in the Andes/Freedom Pure Freedom/ Jeffrey Marcus Oshins - Santa Barbara, Calif.: Deep Six Publishers © 2014

p. ; cm.
ISBN: 978-0-9831981-5-4 (ppb) ; 978-0-9831981-4-7 (ebook) 978-8987788-1-4) (hardback)
Summary: *Hippies in the Andes* is a road story where Jeffrey Marcus Oshins and Jeremy Gold take off from California in 1974 to travel by land to visit Filipe Jolly-Luque in Buenos Aires. Stopping in Quito to pick up Jonathan Klontz, the three endure long bus rides, perform rock and roll songs for Indians, are jailed in Chile after hiking with smugglers through the snowbound wastes of the high Andes. *Freedom Pure Freedom,* a fictional version of the same story with some of the same characters, imagines a reverse Peace Corps where a poor Indian farmer is brought to the United States.

1. Jeffrey Marcus Oshins (author)--Non-Fiction. 2. Travel -- Non-Fiction. 3. Adventure -- Non-Fiction. 4. Hippies -- Non-Fiction. 5. Latin America.-- Non-Fiction. 6. 1974 -- Non- Fiction. 7. Latin American culture -- Non-Fiction. 8. Santa Barbara. California -- Non-Fiction. 8. Marijuana -- Non-Fiction. 9. Rock and Roll -- Non-Fiction. 10.. U.S. Government -- Fiction. 10. International Aid -- Fiction. 11. Peace Corps -- Fiction.

Cover art: Ernesto Jolly

Praise for the 12 series of novels by Jeffrey Marcus Oshins

12: A Novel About the End of the Mayan Calendar
&
And We Shall Perish

Never a dull moment, this was a hard-to-put-down, exciting tale written by a talented author.

5 star Amazon review
–Shell Forest Melody

The novel 12 is filled with magic, fantastic visions, invented words, chase scenes through mountain lakes in the Sierras and school campuses...and even music: A CD by Oshins' band Apokaful, which is also the name of a band playing at a nightclub in the novel...(Apokaful is an adjective describing someone who is preoccupied with thoughts of the end of the world.)

–Santa Barbara Independent

If you're looking for the standard doom-and-gloom world-ending catastrophic calendar-end story--look somewhere else, this is not it.

–4 star Amazon review
Mallory Anne-Marie Haws

12 *is a beautifully written, remarkably original book.*

–David B. Stockwell
Author of Tanks in the Wire

Thanks to Oro, J.K., and Jolly for some of the best times I've ever known.

Foreword

The original idea is to visit Felipe Jolly Luque in Buenos Aires. Blind naïveté and magical protection of white Americans, we step off the plane in Quito and are gone, out of reach, six-month, 12,500 miles overland through plastic-free cultures on the eve of globalization.

Chilean college students hide from their generals in cheap hotels. Smugglers abandon me in the high Argentine Andes. Night, dead of winter, alone through snowbound passes, I find my way into Chile to be arrested for illegal entry and possession of pot.

Freedom Pure Freedom is a fictional version of the trip and a homage to my father who dies weeks after I finish this. I imagine a reverse Peace Corp–he certainly could have originated–by which a Peruvian campasino is sent to the United States.

Handwritten, a time capsule, I use a light hand to identify people, reform chapters, grammar and spelling.

Meet my younger self, innocence and hope, music and friends, faith in fellow travelers.

Jeffrey Marcus Oshins

Santa Barbara, 2023

Setting Off

Friday, April 5, 1974, my 24th birthday I started the trip to South America. John Wynn, (my roommate freshman year at Menlo College), was visiting me at this time. Woke up at 4:00 a.m. finished packing, took off at sunrise. I picked up Jerry (Jeramy Gold, my traveling companion) and headed (from Santa Barbara) for Long Beach in the Pinto. It was hard saying good-bye to my father who was so close to death. I fully expected that was the last time I would see him. I was glad to be proven wrong upon my return six months later.

We drove to Long Beach in festive spirits. John W. is very happy with his monkish service to Guru Maharaj Ji. As long as he feels fulfilled I approve. The purpose of going to Long Beach was twofold: (1) We were to get a free yellow fever inoculation at Public Health by the wharf, and (2) to learn about tires so Jerry and I could sell them in South America for Davies International Import-Export. Davies was this man who bought the Rover from me and when he heard about the trip enlisted me to find business for him in South America. Our sojourn to the tire plant was really quite hilarious. We all were on such a free and easy trip and suddenly found ourselves learning the ins and outs of the tire trade. On to Long Beach where we took care of some health matters. Then on to L.A. Int. Airport where I caught a flight to San Francisco for a visit with Nana and

Author setting off April 1974 to travel through the Andes

Geep, my grandparents.

Jerry, my would-be traveling partner, almost backed out at the airport. Jerry and I did not know each other. He was a friend of my brother Steve's (Stephen Oshins, my "Irish twin" 13 months younger than me). And running around L.A. all day plus Jerry just having some teeth extracted (god he looked funny with his mouth all swollen and hair cut so short like Dustin Hoffman's ugly brother), plus the confusion of when and how we were going to meet plus I think John and I were flipping him out by having such a good time in L.A., left him saying at one point that he would wait till summer and come down with someone else. I never took him too seriously because I knew how much he was up for the trip. There was also the matter that I wanted to fly to Quito because Jon Klontz (a high school friend from the American International School of Vienna), was studying there and Gary (Sangenitto) and Marsea (Kieser)—friends and housemates from college—were going to meet me there. Since Jerry did not know these people, he was unsure of whether he wanted to start the trip in Ecuador. In the end we decided to meet the following Thursday at Miami Int. Airport. I was going to fly to Florida for a short visit with Roger Stanley (my "best" friend growing up in Virginia), and meet Jerry in Miami and fly to Quito.

Jerry took the car back to S.B. which must have been funny since he left that morning with all his stuff not to return for many months.

Hi, I'm back —10 hours later.

Joey (Averback) picked John up at the airport and I tried to get on a plane to S.F. in spite of a strike. I made it and arrived at N&G's late that night. Very wired and buzzing with the expectations of what was to come.

On Sunday, Steve came over for dinner at N&G's or rather to join us for dinner at the Club (Peninsula Country Club, San Mateo). All were in excellent spirits and we had a fine meal with many extra helpings as only the Club can provide. Geep laid some money on me that Steve owed me and I read some books on South America and made arrangements with Delta Airlines. Night-flight to Atlanta, connection to Gainesville to see Roger, then Miami-Quito-Miami.

After dinner, Steve and I took the bus to Berkeley where Steve laid a backpack and assorted camping things on me.

I had bought new shoes, Pavetta 5's, and Jerry and I had gone in on a tent together. I had a good time with Steve. We both get along best when we're going places and doing things. It's only when we get bogged down together someplace that he's hard to get along with.

I took the bus back to the airport and just barely caught the plane

Early Monday morning, I arrived in Atlanta. Made my connection on the Eastern flight to Gainesville. On the plane I happened to pick up this magazine about fancy houses around the country. I was surprised to find many were in or around S.B. I like S.B. a lot not only for living but it's a nice place to return to.

I got to Gainesville and hitchhiked to Roger's apartment but he wasn't there. I waited around outside until this very attractive girl whom I had seen riding a bike came up to the apartment and went in. I asked for Rog and found out he had gone home but was expected back any moment. He arrived as I was showering and we had a great reunion after five years. He was my best friend for so long it was easy to glide right back into a friendship.

We proceeded on a four-day binge of dissipation.

Gainesville is a college town and Rog is well known at all the bars. He is a very talented musician but lost all his equipment on a bad deal. While I was there he got in a new band but he's on a hard road now and doesn't practice. Would like to have him out here in a band with me. But that will only happen if I can sell some songs I've written. Before I left, Martin (Sensiper) and I had talked of going to the Club Med and had even written and called France but it never worked out. Roger was in on the deal. It would have been nice playing together on some island somewhere. Perhaps later. "Now I want to go to South America," I thought to myself.

Thursday the 11th April, Roger, his girlfriend and I drove down to see his parents. It was fine seeing them again. This time as friends and not as parents always telling us what to do. Barbara, Roger's little sister came over very pregnant and her husband, some ex-con frustrated racecar driver, drove us high-speed to the Tampa Airport where I caught a flight to Miami where Jerry was supposed to be waiting.

We met up okay, bought tickets, made last minute phone calls. And at 3:30 a.m. of the 12th, took off on Ecuadorian (Airlines) for Quito.

I slept for an hour or two and woke as we were flying over Panama. I saw the canal from the window and we landed for a half hour in Panama City; then we flew to a stop in Cali and then Quito. We got off the plane and there we were, Indians and all.

We tried but could not find any trace of the Centro Andino or Jon Klontz. The people at the information desk recommended a hotel. We caught a cab, left my coat, went back, lost my coat. First lesson—watch your stuff. If you take your eye off it, it will certainly be liberated. We were driven to a small hotel, rather a nice place for what we would come to be accustomed to in S.A. To take a hot shower you had to turn on an electric heater attached to the shower head. I was sure I was going to electrocute myself. But at the time seemed like the lowest dive I had ever seen, much less stayed in.

We were shown to the dungeon with fungus on the wall, damp and bug infested. I balked and was feeling the ol' culture shock. We asked for another room and were led upstairs and just as I was thinking how am I ever going to communicate with anyone down here, this cat pops his head out of a door wearing a Grateful Dead tee-shirt and thus we met Wally and Suzanne.

Though we met many others on our trip, none had quite as profound an influence on us. We were feeling timid and in fear of all that was new around us and Wally, who was something of an old hand, was just the opposite—he enjoyed the feeling of being a head taller than everyone as we all were, and really was overbearing with the Indians. But that kind of confidence was contagious and my fear and inhibition soon dissipated or were at least balanced by some of Wally's bravado.

He recognized the address of the Centro Andino and agreed to show us over that afternoon. The owner of the "Hilton" (the real name) showed us a room, but as Jerry was attempting to discuss the matter with her, I wandered up the stairs and found a nice patio with a great view of the beautiful verdant hills and snow and cloud-capped mountains of Quito. I was anxious to try our new dome tent so we got a good deal for 25 sucre with meals and set up our tent on the roof and christened it the penthouse. It turned out to be a fine place. We got some chairs and a table up there and had many a fine party.

The Hilton had an old guitar which I played up there at first hesitantly but when W & S and Jerry liked it so much I got more confidence. I have since decided that the U.S. is so inundated with excellent musicians and music that a live performance of someone of my competence is sneered at and it amazes me that anyone ever has the encouragement to go on to higher levels of performance of original materials. It's all big money and big concerts that put musicians in a position that's so grand and loud that they must feel super egotistical but what happens in between? Whereas in South America where there are no (rock)concerts, little (top 40-type) radio, a rank amateur like myself if he is carrying a guitar, as I did, is often asked to play. At first I had remnants of my old lack of confidence from the U.S. caused by lack of encouragement but down in SA I received fantastic response whenever I played and so discovered the joy of playing music for those who truly enjoy it. There were also moments of weirdness when I would be playing for a group of people and they would start talking. If I were playing a gig I guess I would just start up another song, but in the context of a small group I felt I had to lower my energies and consciousness from a playing level to a conversational-party frame of mind and it was hard for me to bounce back and forth.

On Monday we went over to the Centro Andino, having found no one about all weekend. The Centro Andino is an extension of the University of New Mexico and Jon Klontz was supposed to be there. We found out that though the rest of the students had returned from their spring vacation on Monday, Jon was not expected back until the next day. He had gone to Bogotá. So we left a note for him and went to the post office to leave word for Gary & Marsea. I found mail for them which showed that they had not yet passed back through Quito. I left notes for them and set out to see the city. Though I had been there for two days already, I was just beginning to feel comfortable.

Quito is approx. 9,500 feet in the air and situated within 40 miles of the equator, thus the sun is very intense and the temp mild. At midday as I roamed through the narrow steep hills the city seemed to shimmer in the glare of the sun. There are a minority of whites in the population and as in the other Indian countries we were to visit, they live in a modern commercial fashion, control the resources and are the social elites. After them come the "mestizos," the Indians with white ancestors, and finally the vast majority of the population, the various Indians. The Indians are generally very poor and live in the country. Most live outside the economy and trade their crops for other goods. The next upward economic level is the Indians who sell wares; i.e., all kinds of foods and utensils and clothing to each other and for a healthy upkick in price to the gringos (no matter if you're a hippie or a jet setter you're a gringo to the inhabitants of Latin A.). The next group was by far the most interesting to me—the "Otavalos," who are called the Jews of

Ecuador. They retain their cultural identity with long braided hair, white calf-length pants and most distinctive, their poncho, blue on one side and plaid on the other. I was told they are found all over the world looking the same and selling their beautiful products. I was not surprised to see them in Bogotá but having been one of my first Latin America experiences, it was almost too ironic when waiting in a L.A. (Los Angeles) bus terminal for the last leg home I saw one boarding a bus for San Francisco. That was truly a fitting and symmetrical sight for my last South American experience of the trip six months later.

I was at first paranoid about the food, having heard stories of incessant bowel woes and ruined trips. I later was to get sick but at first I was too overcautious. One night after dinner we were walking home and Wally by his own misbehavior got into a slight altercation with some men. He was very belligerent and we dragged him off before he hurt someone. That was the only trouble we ever experienced of that sort on the whole trip. You get the vibes you put out as a lady bus driver in Oakland once told me.

The next morning while sunning on the roof Jon appeared, and I was most glad to see him as he was an old friend from Vienna and Washington and knew more of South America than anyone else I knew in the world.

We partied with Jon and waited for Gary & Marsea, I was also slowly slipping into the vastly interesting, ever changing but mellow lifestyle of traveling in South A. Though everything and everybody around us was a new and unique experience, the pace of life was markedly slower and more easy going than the U.S. & Europe.

Particularly the form and type of experience I encountered. In the U.S. I'm often overdosed. A party or a concert will be just too much input, too much going on then sleep and up for another party or high pressure work day. But in L. America there are always new and fascinating things to involve yourself with, but somehow they're more apparent or firsthand and tangible than orgy-like illusionary diversionistic life of the U.S. Like every town in L.Am. has a central square where the people congregate to walk, talk or get out of the house. So by just sitting in a park in a very mellow fashion the people would come and talk or just walk by you. I often had some of my most pleasurable moments and enlightening experiences sitting peaceably on a bench. For similar reasons my mind seemed to grow less cluttered and more capable of clearer thinking. I talked less at first, mostly because I knew no Spanish, and as all the superfluous information that was constantly being pumped into my head by commercials, classes and songs slipped into my unconscious I found myself able to write music, hear and understand myself better and grew to feel more comfortable with myself. I am sure that if I had not had Jerry and Jon or was not meeting new people all the time I would have grown increasingly introverted but as it was, society and self struck a comfortable balance for me and I found South Am. very beautiful and culturally fascinating.

We waited throughout the week for Gary and Marsea but Jerry was wanting to push on with Wally & Suzanne. The Walrus, as we called Wally, had had it with Quito. He had come to play basketball on a team in Quito. We had gone to a practice and a game with him. Earlier that day we had played Frisbee in a park and had attracted a crowd who oohed and aahed at our catches. A few tried to throw it but were incapable which made our performance that much more amazing to them. We enjoyed that so much that during the halftime we went on to the basketball court and started playing catch with the Frisbee. The crowd went nuts. Jerry caught one between his legs and caught a standing ovation. The basketball team came out of the lockers to see what was happening. To be sure we were the hit of the evening. I tried to play a little basketball but the altitude was so high that I was exhausted after five minutes.

By Thursday, I had about decided to leave. Gary and Marsea had not shown up and Jerry was anxious to leave with the Walrus & Suzanne for the Port of Guayaquil. I made arrangements to meet Jon in La Paz the 10th of June, packed up and got as far as the taxi Friday morning. The plan was to go to Riobamba for a festival that weekend then on to Guayaquil. Just as I was stepping into the cab I decided to stay the weekend and take the Tuesday train to Guayaquil.

That afternoon Jon and I left to go to Ibarra, north of Quito, where Jon had to interview some people about this project he was doing on a small village of blacks north of the town. Ecuador is a country of mountains and jungles. The lands north of Quito are a patchwork of green fields and furrowed pastures where the Indians farm often with primitive methods on the sides of mountains at incredibly steep angles usually far from any road or neighbor. It's as if Kansas in the spring got pulled up the side of the Rockies. So we left for Ibarra and points north, my first day on the road.

Country towns are much more the domain of the native populations than the capital cities of South America, which are the bastion of the elites. Like the rest of the world, the capitals are the Oz of those poor who desert their meager existence in the country for the promise of the cities. It is a story often seen in history. Rome too, I am sure, had and still does if I recall its slums—a shanty town to breed and die in. A few get jobs as cheap laborers or servants but many, perhaps most, struggle to survive day by day without hope of relief. No, the capital cities of L.Am. are an anomaly in many ways. The riches of the elites are totally out of keeping and the poverty of the barrios just as hopeless as in the country. Perhaps there is more hope in the cities, a slim chance to move up. Perhaps that's what attracts people there from the country. Dad thinks it's on account of the country being so boring—at least the city has crowds and lights. The poverty of a L.Am. city is different than in the U.S. You can sleep on the street, as many do, particularly before a market day, and a meal can be begged or a taco sold.

On Saturday I saw my first market in Ibarra. Most of the population of the Andean countries and Central America live outside of the economy, as we know it. They grow enough for themselves to eat and a little to trade or barter. Thus the incredibly low per capita income figures of $250-$500 per year. Also in the market are factory-made goods such as pots, pans and plastics. An Indian market is a whirl of action starting up early in the morning and going until night though most of the buying is done in the morning.

Some markets, of which Ibarra is one, have finely made clothing that attracts tourists. The attraction of Ibarra was Otavalos ponchos (the town Otavalo is just down the road) and embroidered shirts, both of which I'm sorry to say went unpurchased by J.O. On the way up we did stop in one town, Calderón, which specialized in little dough figures of which I bought one and gave to Suzanne. Sunday, Jon and I took the bus to San Antonio de Ibarra whose specialty was wood. I bought a wooden necklace for about 25 cents—it must have taken hours to make. Jon and I talked of how much one could make if he imported these—while it would be good for the Indians it would be a good mini-example of how the U.S. absorbs so much of the world's products. Though I know Jon would be more considerate of the Indians than a big company, the truth shown is that the U.S. controls the wealth or contains the wealth of most of the world. I have not figured out whether the Indians are doomed to poverty forever or if there is hope, but today a man works his whole life and receives nothing and is lucky if he can survive while I do no work and I am in a position to buy his products. I'm not in favor of radical political changes because as Chile and history show, radical changes cause much suffering, but I hope to see in my life the poor of the world given better opportunities than they have today to grow and reap a better life from their labors.

Oro hitchhiking not likely to get a ride here even naked

Miracle in Quito

Upon my return Monday morning I found the "miracle" had happened: G & M were in Quito. And was I glad to see them. It was fortunate I had decided to stay because they arrived that Saturday. Sometimes I think I'm insensitive to where people are at. It was obvious that G & M were very worn out and at the end of their trip. Marsea said it, "Your trip is just beginning." It made no sense for us to travel together. I finally realized this and stopped insisting that they extend their trip. We had a good day together and in the morning I was up at 4:00 and off to Guayaquil on the *autofaril*.

It was interesting to see G & M. It was also a bit of a shock. Genteel Marsea looked like a Haight Street panhandling sleeze chick but Gary didn't look too different/skinnier.

The trip to Guayaquil went through the mountain where I saw villages similar to pictures I had seen of Africa with grass thatched huts. Then we dropped down to the jungle down a steep grade where the *autofaril* (which is really a bus on tracks) had to back down switchbacks at some points—very steep grade. As we passed little towns and villages I realized that paved streets and modern conveniences are only for the big cities. Life in the country is hard.

Guayaquil is a big port, hot and humid. I took the boat across the dank delta waters of the river. It is a very commercial city and could be quite interesting if it were not so humid. I met up with Jerry. The Walrus and Suzanne were flying that night to Panama and we decided to beat the humidity and beat it on down to Cuenca. We had our first bad experience with directions given; got four directions on how to get to the bus but finally made it and had our first good "funky bus" (a conveyance built for Hobbits, not for men) ride along a winding mountain road.

Cuenca is a beautiful old colonial city with a stream running through it. We spent a week there. My wallet got picked in the market but the karma was too strong. I've had that wallet since high school and the thief couldn't handle it—he gave it back to me saying it had fallen out of my pocket. The fact that it had no money in it helped too, I believe. A great wallet impossible to lose, I think I shall soon have to retire it.

While in Cuenca, as was our habit throughout the trip, we endeavored to meet some of the womenfolk. While walking down these old wide and banking steps to the river we were passed by several groups of giggling girls who responded to our smiles with paroxysms of more giggles. Thus encouraged, we managed to engage a young blonde by the university in a conversation of sorts.

Jerry was endeavoring to practice his Spanish. While my Spanish vocabulary had grown by five times from two to ten, I sat back and tried to look interested. Just as it appeared that I was never to get a word in, I remembered my Berlitz phrase book had a section on how to chat up a bird. So there I come out of a stone silence with the worse accent asking her to go to the movies.

In great apprehension I awaited a response to my first question ever in Spanish and got instead a blank look of non-comprehension. So I showed her the book and she blushed prettily and explained that she would never be permitted to go to a movie with a strange man.

Later on she invited us home where we met her family. Jerry was a bit uncomfortable because he had to do all the talking but I enjoyed the experience of seeing a household. The lessons I learned were 1) the father is king, 2) the woman is either a whore or a housewife. Though we were to later see women in the lower echelons of banks and airlines, their roles are much more limited than in the States.

There were six girls in this family and our visits were occasions for lessons from the mother on how to deal with gentlemen callers and perspective beaus. It was all very genteel and reminiscent of the Old South. Jerry and I decided that most any woman, if your credentials were in order, would marry you and be a model wife, raise the kids and be respectable while you played with your mistresses.

They had an Indian servant girl named Blanca—she's the only name I can remember—and we thought what a crack up if suddenly we told the mother that we wanted to ask for someone's hand for marriage in her household and then asked Blanca. They probably would just laugh so you'd have to go through with it to pull it off. Even the fact that we said hi and smiled at Blanca caused something of a stir.

On the day that we were to leave for Peru I was feeling sick and stayed in bed for the morning. I got up to brush my teeth and left my bag in the washroom. Naturally, five minutes later when I returned it was gone. I got very mad and almost lit into this idiot who was standing around 'cause I thought he had it. They called the police and I think I might have gotten it back if we didn't have to catch a bus.

Next followed a hard trip. By morning I was feeling a bit better and we got to Peru. But at the border they made us buy these jive tickets out of the country. We argued about that for a few hours and finally complied but by that time it was too late to catch the bus to Lima so we spent the night in Tumbes—what a pit.

It was there that I wrote "Culture Shock Blues."

"Me and Oro went riding south
Find out what it's all about
Here's now what we found out.
Baby's crying
Chickens flying.
Old man looks like he's dying.
I just want to go home.
Cause I got them, yes I've got them, I've got them
Homesick blues."

I was disgusted and that was certainly the low point of the trip. In the morning we were to take a 24-hour bus ride which at the time seemed impossibly long to me.

We were later to take trips of five days or more. Fortunately the bus was comfortable (an old Greyhound that still had Harrisburg on top as its destination). We got good seats up front and stretched out.

We drove down the coast of Peru on the Pan American Highway

which is the only paved highway in Peru. The coast is a complete desert except for an oasis here and there—totally barren. Since there was little scenery to watch we amused ourselves by playing the harmonica and kazoo, both great crowd pleasers as we had discovered in Ecuador.

Jerry and I talked about what we would do with our lives. We actually suffer from too many choices, quite different from the people around us who usually do what their father did or something similar without a range of choice. Jerry and I decided that in the end we would probably do whatever presented itself at the time. J.G. talked about taking some money and starting an import-export deal. But he will never do that. He couldn't even handle the Davies Int. trip. Though I can't really blame him. It's ridiculous for us to go talk to a Latino businessman after having lived out of a backpack for three months. Everyone (the businessmen and elites) dresses up down there to show how American they are and how un-Indian. We were just the opposite, we would wear Indian clothes—the result being a little weird when we tried to do some business. We did make a contact in Quito but found out later that they went bankrupt. We used to joke about making some money but it never really was anything more than a joke. Right before we left, J.G. had just had his wisdom teeth pulled and was swollen up so that it was painful to laugh. We went over to see Davies and he was going on about how much we could make. Jerry was struggling successfully through that but when Davies brought out a box of about 1,000 business cards with my name printed on them in gold, he blew it and in his struggle to keep from laughing looked for all the world like his head was going to explode. So, from the whole business end of the trip, it was a bit absurd.

I had a good night's sleep on the bus or better than I thought I would and woke to find us fast approaching the rising spires of Lima. When we arrived a cat we'd met on the bus took us to a place where I called Manongo Mojica, an old friend from Vienna. He comes from an old and respected family and I had to call the family office to find out where he was. He was married and his father, who had been the Peruvian ambassador in Vienna, had died. I saw Manongo and his sister that afternoon and we drove to a beautiful beach and had a beer. Lima is an oasis surrounded by desert and dunes. Though it often gets foggy there, the weather was nice throughout our stay.

Manongo was still into music and had played with the Rolling Stones Organization in London. He left when the guitar player smashed the bass player over the head with his guitar in the studio. Apparently they had the same manager as the Stones and he provided them with the best equipment and hash but no food—thought the adversity would do them good as it did in the early days of the Stones.

We spent a good deal of time in Miraflore—the fancy part of town. In Lima, if you're a hippie, you're rich—no one else could afford to grow long hair and hang out in the rich part of town. After a week we decided to go on to Cuzco. We looked on a map and found that there was a route through the mountains via Abancay but were told at a few places that route was closed. Besides, the route via Arequipa though long, was more comfortable. Either way the trip took from 2-4 days depending on breakdowns, landslides, etc. Indicative of traveling conditions down there was the trip to Cuzco from Lima. There was a tourist jet that cost $50 one way and got you there in an hour—or the way most of our friends went by paved road to Arequipa in the very south and then by train to Puno than by bus to Cuzco so the route looks like a triangle.

Well we took a bus that was going straight across. That was my true initiation into the ranks of hard-core traveling. For two days and nights we sat on this little Indian bus that was crammed to the brim with Indians and their belongings.

The first part along the coast to Ica was paved but that was short-lived. We changed buses and took off on an unpaved road into the mountains and the night. While waiting to change buses we went into this café where I played guitar and was served pisco, a drink similar to tequila and very tasty.

What a night! Somehow I got some sleep. We were sitting right on the wheel and every bump shot right through my cramped body. By the end of the trip I was convinced the ol' bod had suffered permanent damage.

At nightfall of the second day we were forced to stop at a landslide. That had been an amazing day and adventures and sights seemed to flow into each other and merge. Here we were stuck at a jungle stream, while early that morning I had awoke at dawn to find us crossing a high plain that swept to the jagged snow-capped Andes. It was the beginning of winter and as I walked from the bus through the frozen tundra, I experienced for the first time the eerie echo of complete silence that is characteristic of the Altiplano. Wild llama-like animals, vicuña, and llama grazed in herds in the distance and though they were far away the cool crisp rarefied air brought them into a unique perspective, and the echoes of the endless plains brought the imaginary sound of a hoof falling to my ears still ringing with the sounds of civilization of which now only the bus remained.

That day we climbed, traversed and fell through treacherous winding dirt roads till finally the landslide.

All the machos on the bus got out to start hacking away at the dirt with shovels. J & I soon realized that the magnitude of the slide made that impossible so we climbed on top of the slide to watch the fun. One terribly fat man floundered in the mud and looked all the world like a beached whale. That brought the house down and since quite a crowd had gathered, there was no dearth of other misadventures to keep us amused.

The landslide had occurred right before a bridge. On one side of the bridge was a bus of the same company as ours going to Lima. Well putting our ol' Yankee ingenuity to its best advantage we suggest a switch and we would all be on our way. At first the idea seemed to be taking hold but alas bureaucracy is the same the world over—totally incapable of accommodating innovation. So that night most slept in the bus. J.G. did, but I found a small beach along the raging river, which would have been very nice and was, in any case, more comfortable than the bus on account I could stretch my legs out, but my sleeping gear was stowed on top of the bus and I had to sleep without benefit of my Insulite sleeping pad, but it was okay.

In the morning trouble struck in the form of little yellow flies that suck your blood and leave horrible itchy bites. We were eaten alive. Nowhere to hide, Jerry wrapped his face up in a sweater but since it was so hot that was a bit uncomfortable. I took a sheet I had around my guitar and dipped it in the river before wrapping it all around me. Insect repellent worked a bit.

But when we finally left, aided by a bulldozer, everyone was covered with scarlet bites. There were Indians who live there so I guess one can adapt but it would be hell to live amongst those beasts for long.

Late that night the excitement that had been building in the bus reached a crescendo as we rounded one last peak and there lying below were the lights of Cuzco. For many of the people on the bus this was the end of the longest trip of their lives and for me the end of the hardest, so my feelings of relief flowed with the general ambiance of happiness on the bus.

The bus trip was the most arduous I've ever taken or want to take again. But even with the acute discomfort, the scenery I saw—the mountains, animals, lands and people—were so magnificent and beyond anything I had ever imagined could exist, I stumble on coherent thoughts that sleep in my memories and rise again in a sharp glacial peak jumping from the mountains and falling to the depths as the bus wound through snake dirt roads following river bed cut deep and low. I start a quick exclamation and wonder at the reality I just perceived.

We found a place to stay and I suffered through the night scratching my bites and longing for some calamine lotion. In the morning I walked out into the brilliant sunlight of an Andean morning, got my calamine lotion and proceeded to check out the town.

Nana and Geep, my grandparents, had warned me about too

much activity in Cuzco the first day on account of the altitude, but having ridden on the bus I was all but acclimated or should I say acaltituded.

Cuzco is a strange admixture. It is the one place in South America that I believe is the most famous tourist attraction. Every sort of tourist arrives there—mostly by jet—or by way of Arequipa. Cuzco is the remains of the Inca capital sacked by the Spaniards. More than Rome or Athens vibrating still with its once glorious past. In no way was I prepared for the glory of the Saksaywaman, the ruins in or around Cuzco. Europe has so much cultural hype that by the time I saw the Parthenon I had seen it in so many pictures that I was prepared for the eventual sight, but the mammoth stones and winding trails of the Inca civilization were hitherto unbeknownst to me and were thus incredibly more impressive and left that much more of an initial impact on me.

Cuzco is inhabited mostly by tourists and Indians. We saw more gringo concentrated there than in any other spot. The people of Cuzco make many fine woven bags and ponchos and the market there is fascinating to wander through.

We had been told of a vegetarian restaurant by Manongo. While eating there we were told of another vegetarian restaurant which was to have music that night. One of the things I missed most on the trip was music. It is a large part of my life in the States—perhaps too much in that my ears are constantly being pounded with everything from advertisement jingles to rock concerts. But to go from incessant music to scarcely none left me going into music stores just to listen to records. I also love to play with people and in that respect my guitar was a great boon but even though Gary had mentioned such a place—a club with Marshal amps he said, I was still amazed to find this club the "Samana" packed with about $10,000 worth of equipment—bass, guitars, amps, drums, P.A., the works. Well I got to be friends with these people and we ended up staying there for two weeks sleeping on the floor. Jerry didn't like it, but I was in with the musicians of Cuzco and enjoyed playing with them everyday. Jerry felt that the people had a hipper-than-thou attitude about everyone else who came through and admitted the place was an anomaly in the middle of the Andes full of Europeans and hip Peruvians—quite a scene but enjoyable for me nonetheless. I used to despise the rest and relaxation fancy hamburgerville Bergtesgarten in Germany, but now I realize that the Samana was a similar experience for me. Though it was a scene I was not comfortable in, it still smacked of familiarity and, outside of everything else, there was the music. But then everyone in the place started coming down with hep.

I had been feeling weak and had gotten a cold from trying some snow. I don't know why everyone makes a big deal about cocaine. I think it's hype. In its pure form it hurts the nose and makes me feel all speedy and rushed out. People in the U.S. get a much impure form, cut with god knows what, and I think they like it more for the luxury or social significance than for what it does to them. In a way, snow is like alcohol—you have to learn to like it, find a special place in your mind and body to tolerate. I disliked both the first time I tried them and see no reason to go to the extreme expense (in the U.S.) and danger of procuring cocaine and disrespecting my body.

I did once succumb to cigarettes but if I had ever listened to my body the first time I would never have touched them. If you listen to your body, it will tell you what you need.

Well, the scene at the Samana was getting a bit hairy with everyone getting sick and Jerry was wanting to leave. One night I became very sick with shaking and high fever. It was probably caused by a virus, but at the time I was afraid of hepatitis, the scourge of that area and all poor countries.

The next morning I felt better and we moved to another hotel. I got a shot of gamma globulin. There is a general popular belief that this drug does not help but it put me back on my feet in a few days, and I insisted that Jerry get one too in that there was a good chance that he had gotten in contact with the hep.

Though I was sick, I did get to see Sacsayhuamán, the ruins above Cuzco. Mammoth black stone parade marching ground of a past empire, built of materials transported hundreds of miles over mountains without the aid of the wheel. Giant stones cut and laid by master stone masons in an art now lost. How did they do it? Certainly not with the technology we presume them to have.

As soon as I was sufficiently recovered, we decided to leave for Machu Picchu—the wonder of the world.

By this time my money was about out. I had written Dad to wire me money in La Paz but that was a week or more away. So in an effort to economize and also in respect to the "reverse snobism" we were developing and likewise because it was bound to be more interesting, we decided to take the Indian train to Machu Picchu.

Machu Picchu

Now for a dollar you can take this trip where the fancy train cost $10. It's not that much more comfortable, you're just assured a seat and assured that the Indians you see will not be sharing your seat with you—very separated and detached from the realities of country which seems to be the way most tourists see S.A. Thus the "reverse snobism." I felt that our efforts and sickness on account of trying to live down closer to the people were paying off and earning us a feeling of superior awareness. Certainly this trip on the train earned us another merit badge in our pursuit of awareness. The train left at 5:30 in the morning but we had been warned not to get there any later than 4:00 a.m. or we would never get a seat. So come 4 o'clock there we are, marching to the train.

The station is right in the marketplace of Cuzco and it being the morning of a big market, Saturday, the place was teaming. The train station was packed with Indians hauling everything from bags of flour to goat heads, along the route of the train. We took our place in the ticket line amidst much pushing and shoving, but since we were heads taller than these high-altitude, undernourished people, we were usually able to hold our ground.

At about 5:00 the window opened and we got our tickets. By now the place was packed. We pushed up as close as we could to the locked gate, which opened to the train. We were holding our full packs and as the crowd surged with anticipation we often had to use them as buffers against the hundreds of people surging all around. It was worse than the 5:15 p.m. subway to the Bronx.

And well when those doors finally opened it was like nothing on this earth except perhaps the bull runs at Pamploma. With a great leap, trampling, shoving, jumping, hauling, lifting, the crowds surged through the gates and ran down the platform to the train. Rather than get trampled we swung our packs as bludgeons and powered it on. Charging down the ramp we jumped on a car and everywhere we'd go one man or a child would be trying to save a seat for five others. Finally we said forget it and just sat down to the protests of the fellow trying to stop us. The gimmick is to get one person on and secure a berth then comes the family and luggage, usually a bushel of corn or some such commodity. As it turned out the fellow didn't need our seats and all was well, but it was fortunate that we clamored and scraped as we did for within ten minutes there was a not a seat to be found on the train.

The train was like a moving marketplace—perhaps what Hemingway had in mind when he coined the phrase "a moveable feast" though the train and countryside was a long way from anything Parisian. At every stop women would be selling corn and meat and prepared dishes in and out of the train.

The family across the way from us consisted of the grandmother (the matriarch, chief buyer, and all around boss); her young pretty daughter; the daughter's husband; and their child. They seemed a happy family judging by the playfulness of their young daughter.

They had obviously done well in Cuzco because they were buying out the house—breads, corn, goats heads, a live chicken that kept popping out of the sack. All this activity seemed to swell and bustle out of their beautiful robes.

I had begun to be able to distinguish poorer Indians, though there is no overt class discrimination that I could detect. Any movement from the bare poverty level was an achievement marked by good luck, health, not too many children, and hard work. The amount of children one has down there can often make the difference. The optimal amount is neither what is the popular belief in the U.S.; i.e., as few as you can support or better none. Therefore the massive birth control emphasis. Nor is it the popular conception of the Latino that the more children who survive the richer and more secure shall be the parents. I concluded that it was the belief that children mean senior care, coupled with the macho virility factor that was the cause of outright anti-birth control beliefs, rather than the Catholic Church. While the major factor in their lack of use when made available is their expense and the plain stupidity of the people. I believe that due to generations of malnourishment most people down in the poor countries never obtain their full intellectual capacity and are genuinely quite stupid and incapable of raising their children in a healthy, intelligent way so that they too can't obtain their full potential. It's a vicious cycle and the one factor in my opinion that is most responsible for the lack of the people's ability to organize themselves into better political and social structures. But the Indians are a delightful energetic lot by the most part and I fully enjoyed the ride on that moving market.

There is a four-day hike that can be made into Machu Picchu from "Kilometer 88." Jerry and I had gotten all the maps and had fully planned to make the trek along the old Inca trail, but I was feeling so sick right up until the day that we left that we thought it best to forgo such a strenuous exercise. We did march up the old trail to the top of the ruins. The train lets you off in the valley and though the old city is right on top of you, it is impossible to see it from the gorge. It is for this reason that the city was not discovered by the Spanish and managed to avoid the sacking and destruction that was the fate of Cuzco and Quito and the other pre-Colombian cities of Latin America.

Machu Picchu is a miracle—a wonder of the world. Nothing I had ever read or imagined prepared me for these ruins, thus upon entering them I experienced profound disbelief, utter amazement and actually found myself considering such possibilities as extra-terrestrial intervention. That a civilization that did not even possess the technology of the wheel, had shaped and moved such monstrous rocks, had designed such enduring structures by hand alone seems utterly impossible. Throughout our days there we found ourselves pondering such theses as anti-gravity and where the spaceships had moored themselves. Whatever the source, I am convinced that the people possessed secrets. At least the secret of masonry that were hidden from the Spanish and have yet to be rediscovered by modern science.

After the climb up I was still wasted from being sick and spent the afternoon sitting and marveling at the wonders around me—the high jagged peaks and volcanoes of the Andean jungle mountains, the rushing rivers, and waterfalls in the distance and then the stone ruins around me. We walked out of Machu Picchu proper and found a crag in the mountainside where we could survey the scene. My imagination saw spaceship docking points between two peaks, a mountain peak city of ancient Indian kings, a last retreat from the ravages of the savage Spanish sacking their land and ruining their culture. I imagined the slow decline as the population dropped, and then a final pestilence, the departure of the last survivors leaving the city to ruin and legend. Then a punk professor from Yale following some coke chewing guide up the river and over the ledge to be the first modern witness to the grandeur of Machu Picchu. If Olympus ever existed it had its twin in Peru.

That night we walked back down, a trip of five miles or so, and pitched the tent in a field by the river. In the morning we rode back to the top on the tourist buses and took off to climb Wayna Picchu, the big peak behind the city. From the bottom it looks inaccessible but the Inca had done terrace farming off the side of it, as they had around the city. There is little flat land for cultivation within the city and the people supported themselves primarily by building terraces on the mountain sides, yet even these were undetectable from the valley below. The city would have to have been self-sufficient so every bit of accessible space was used in this manner.

Climbing up Wayna Picchu was like climbing a giant ladder. The Incas had carved and worn down steps and handholds in the rock so that at times you were climbing straight up. The effort was more than paid off by the view. At the pinnacle we sat among the rocks pondering the forces of nature that rose and cut through such mountains and at the adaptability of man who carved a niche for himself and left his monuments for us to gaze at far below.

That afternoon we were surprised to discover that there was no Indian train back to Cuzco and we did not have the funds for the tourist train. The train to Puno was leaving early in the morning from Cuzco so we were in a bit of a fix. We finally managed to stow away on a student train. Got back to Cuzco, changed money at the tourist hotel and caught the train to Puno.

This was certainly the most beautiful and interesting train ride I have ever taken. The train slowly climbed through the high plains reaching heights of 14,000 feet and more through frozen tundra, herds of llama, small villages, lakes and streams. Off to the sides peaks rose to snow-crested heights of 15, 16, 17,000 feet, perhaps even higher. At any point along the vast uninhabited reaches one could take off and climb by foot or horse into the distance and backpack into country rarely visited if ever at all. A stream could be found and followed to a glacial lake where fish would certainly abound. It would be rough going, very cold at night, but adequately prepared, it would be no worse than the High Sierras, but with no garbage along the way. One would experience it as John Muir must have, having first set eyes on Yosemite. Lovely, foreboding, wild and untouched, endless spaces stretching from horizon to horizon. Then we came to the most phenomenal lake in the world.

Miles in the air a fresh water sea, plowed by big ships and reed boats—Lake Titicaca. A vast fresh water world yet surrounded by parched lands, poor farmers ignorant of the most basic fundamentals of farming—irrigation. It was sad to consider their plight in such a harsh environment. It is such people that the simplest form of aid and education would benefit most dramatically.

We didn't like Puno that much but were forced to stay there on account of having to buy those bogus tickets to Bolivia upon entering the country.

The most interesting thing to do in Puno is a boat trip to the floating islands of the Urus. The Urus are a people who live on islands made of reeds. Until recently, generations had passed since any had gone to the shore. The Urus believe that the lake is their mother and the sun their father. They transport themselves on little reed boats and live on fish that they catch and occasionally a duck or seagull. To reach their island one has to hire a boat at the pier for about $10 for the whole trip.

We had met some other people; Jeff at the top of Wayna Picchu, and Shel, a Peace Corps worker. So we got out there early in the morning and waited around for the others to show up. For awhile it seemed that Jeff was going to pay 150 soles and Jerry and I 100, but soon others started showing up including two Germans and two Argentinians so we had quite a crew. There were a number of boats but we got shuffled to an old wreck.

Well I didn't like the looks of that from the start and began to lobby for another boat. The others just kept piling into the wreck so I tagged along. The crew pushed it out past the hull of the big ship that was soon to sail across the lake. This was the boat that Gary and Marsea had told me about, the one I wanted to take. But we couldn't because we had been forced to buy tickets at the northern border of Peru for the bus to Bolivia.

So we got past the big Bolivian boat and these boogies commence to fire up the engine which was sticking out of the middle of the boat with us all around and wham, rattle, shish, boom, bang the whole floor seemed to explode. I thought the boat was going to shake itself to pieces for sure. The problem it seems was the propeller shaft had detached itself from the universal gear and was bouncing all over the place. The crew worked on that for a bit and, much to my relief, gave up and we headed back for shore.

I thought, "That is certainly that. Now let's find another boat." Upon reaching the shore, I jumped out to do just so, but then the owner of the boat comes charging down the dock, panic written all over his face—"I'm going to lose all that money" and "splash" into the water he jumps, clothes, watch, shoes, all rare articles up in those parts not to be dumped into freezing water lightly. I pitied the poor man, with all his huffing and pushing and cursing at the disjointed prop but I never thought there would be any question about us all abandoning the ship.

That just goes to show how little we know of our fellow men. I was half way to the other boat when I noticed I was not being pursued by a quickly exiting horde. To my dismay the popular consensus was to stay with the wreck if it could be fixed. Much to my discomfort it was somehow patched back together and again we were off to parts unknown, huddled around a smoke-belching engine that threatened to shake us to bits. I for one climbed on the roof and took a bead on the shore measuring points that I might hope to swim to since the boat lacked life preservers. I figured it would take some heroics to avoid loss of life and limb.

Without incident we somehow managed to reach the floating home of the Urus. If Gollum from the Lord of the Rings had a terrestrial or should I say "above earth" abode it would certainly be here. As one can imagine, the Urus are not your average folks, living as they do in the middle of a lake. They survive on creatures of the lake and believe that they are its children, though the Christian church is making some inroads if there were only some roads. They have a floating school which they tow from island to island and kids come from surrounding islands to be educated. It was the only example of positive affirmation—no, I also saw orphanages and hospitals run by American Christians. There is no easy judgement of the people of Christ in South America. There are different sects and attitudes and nationalities just as in the Catholic Church. I saw everything from friars begging in Oaxaca to a lecture on the evils of birth control by a Catholic layman, to tales of great bravery by Brazilian and Chilean priests in the face of great oppression, championing the rights of the Indians, but the rule is usually the church is hand in glove with the elites and oppresses the Indians.

The Urus are now in touch with commercialism and greet you with outstretched hands and a store of their crafts. The guidebook tells you to bring them fruit, and the sight of an orange sets children to moaning and clinging to one's sleeves whilst the ladies either smile benignly from out of their filth or follow us as we walk around islands no bigger than a block and no smaller than a quarter of an acre. One must slosh and wade, as the reeds are only floating not watertight.

Upon returning to shore the rudder on the vessel broke and

sent the boat shooting off into the thick reeds that grew on either side of the boat lanes. We finally made it to shore where we fell upon our knees and thanked God for our deliverance. Not really, but it was with some relief that the last time the engine broke down we were close enough to shore to be towed or swim for it.

Whores

That night we met Jeff Wiggs from the Virgin Islands. We had first encountered him on the top of Wayna Picchu behind Machu Picchu, where he took a picture of us (now on the frontispiece of this book) that I received in the mail six months later in Santa Barbara. If I had one picture for the whole trip, I would want it to be that one. I am grateful for him sending it to me after all that time.

We rode the train with Jeff to Puno. He was on a different type of trip than us. He preferred to stay in fancier hotels and eat at good restaurants. Not that we would not have enjoyed indulging ourselves likewise, but we did not have that much money and were trying to conserve at every opportunity. Where Jeff totally indulged himself was with the whores.

Whoring as you can imagine is a very popular enterprise in such poor countries and Jeff was their most enthusiastic supporter. So when we returned from the trip to the Islands of the Urus, Jeff suggested a round with his favorite ladies. Jerry was all for it as it would be a new experience for him. I had some less than satisfactory previous experiences in Europe so was not in the market, but since I was right there when they decided to go, I went along as an interested observer.

They hailed a taxi and Jeff, who was experienced in these types of misadventures, told the driver exactly what we wanted. So off into the night we drove to the outskirts of the city to a house with the proverbial red light. With high expectations of exotic Peruvian women, we walked in to find at least 20 men including a police officer lined up in front of five doors. We stared in amazement as a completely worn-out looking woman opened a door. The poor lady must have had more business than can possibly be healthy. As a cordial act the queue of men motioned for us to go first. We kindly begged off and went outside where we laughed ourselves silly at what we had just seen. Ah the poor frontier whore!

We had been trying to leave Puno ever since we arrived, lamenting that we couldn't take the fantastic old boat train that sails overnight to Bolivia. The boat train costs only a bit more than the exaggerated price we had been forced to pay at the border many weeks before in that lowest of spots, Tumbes. Anyway, on the 30th of May, having been in Peru for exactly a month, we managed to get to Bolivia.

The bus company, Pizango, almost drove us to distraction with their delays but they did finally convey us on a beautiful drive around the Lago to La Paz.

The entrance to La Paz is the most spectacular first encounter of a city I have experienced. Even people on the bus, who had made the trip many times and had forewarned us of the impending sight, gasped in amazement with the rest of us as the bus rounded the final bend and the city lay aglow below us. We had been driving along the plains and for miles we had seen this halo of light on the horizon that at times seemed to be moving away from us, but we did finally come to a brink of a sudden and larger valley and there was La Paz, the highest city of its size in the world.

We found lodging at the Andes Hotel and set out in the morning for American Express. Jerry wanted to go to the bank first but I was starved for mail and dragged him and another friend in my wake to American Express. I found a letter from my brother, Steve, but no more personal mail, but my disappointment at that was more than offset by finding a fantastic document forwarded by Jon Klontz from Ecuador from the Bank of America. In one moment my whole trip changed. Jon said he was coming through on the way to Argentina and the Bank said that I had been endowed with a fresh fund for $250 a month for over a year. I went from being almost broke and wondering how to get home to complete independence to travel wherever I chose.

There was much hand slapping and I knew that I would soon be off to Argentina. At first Jerry thought he wouldn't be able to go but he soon came around. A more immediate problem was whether the funds I had requested had been sent to the local BofA and lo and behold, there they were. It was a great day for financial news. We celebrated by getting a good meal that we had not been able to afford for so long.

Upon a later visit to the American Express I found a letter from Jon saying he would be coming a week late so we settled down for rather a long stay in La Paz.

The letter Steve had written me asked my advice on what he should do with his life, and how school was largely an escape that would soon end. Both of us are artistically talented. He has tremendous potential as a writer. But we have been raised with too many diversions what with school and less legitimate escapes—we lack the confidence to break off from the parental-social life plan which has us doing much more "socially worthwhile endeavors." Personally I know I want to be a musician but cannot convince myself to totally dedicate my life to that pursuit. I am not afraid of failure for in that field every newly written song or newly learned scale is enough satisfaction for me. And as I told Steve, it is possible for me to lose my ego while playing music and flow with the energies of the universe. I attained a state of consciousness akin to meditation where my fingers seemed to act in accord with powers and inspirations that are more finely attuned than anything I could do with my rational conscious state and seems to flow on with the assuredness of a stream—of a stream it has joined and I can float down that stream. On the other half of music is the accomplishment of performing a finely worked out piece, an immaculately precise endeavor of the rational mind.

As I have said I will always have music but I cannot resolve the problem of whether to devote myself full-time to it. I think what with the state of the world and my opportunity to involve myself with government, I will attempt to perform a more temporal service to my fellows than to solely involve myself in what would undoubtedly be the more selfish yet more personally satisfying pursuit of excellence as a musician. However, as I told Steve he should above all follow his artistic gift of writing whenever he can and give his other energies as a valuable gift much needed by himself but begrudgingly donated to society and the betterment of the life of men. But then there is the other side, which argues that what better gift to man than a correct word or meaningful thought or a melodic phrase to wrench the hearts or lighten the load of man.

I do not know which way to go—compromise I suppose. There are no new words or thoughts. Music is dead. Now I must leave my home, my heart's hearth—wander in the cold world the border line of nothing—the last chance. It is my generation's burden to carry on the terrible responsibilities of this country. And if we of peaceful manner and light spirits choose to withdraw into our art who shall control the terrible engines of destruction? Who will they be? Will they be able to see and laugh at folly—tweak the nose of urges that are destructive? Protect and fight for rights of man? Will I?

The military in any country of the world including the U.S. has the power to take over that country by force, and arrest and murder anyone they choose. I saw that in every county I visited. The notion that "can't happen here" is naive. The peace movement met with and was quickly dispersed by the largest armed force in the world. Those who argue that the right to bear arms and the amount of guns in the U.S. will keep us free are arguing a tenuous case. It is true that there would be much resistance and guerilla activity, but what is a hunting rifle against a tank? On the other hand for many years I was against guns and was in favor of abolishing them from society, but now I realize that though they are the cause or part of most heinous crimes, they also act as the only deterrent to an armed takeover of the U.S.

What sort of men and women join the armed forces or police? In past history and in South America, the military was the only route up the social ladder; power, prestige and the defender of the best interest. An automaton obeying the orders of some man of supposedly higher authority killing with no personal guilt if told by the right source.

In the U.S., the armed forces have an honorable tradition and democracy is long standing, but so it was too in Chile. Today I would say the hierarchy of the U.S. military is generally of an unusually enlightened class due to the fact that many of them were drawn from colleges and private business during the war and chose to stay in the military as it was then a dignified and socially accepted role. Today however, after the Vietnam war, police and military are regarded with scorn and considered by most colleagues of a liberal and humanitarian nature to be an onerous profession and shunned as being dishonorable and socially unacceptable. Twenty years ago a college lad like myself would expect and respect a number of his friends who went into the armed services. Today the situation is reversed and we are at a critical point in our history. In our fear we have armed a segment of our society with the most sophisticated weapons leaving little hope in my mind such a group will refrain from using the tremendous power they have been given in any other way than they see fit.

Anyway, back to the trip. La Paz is a very high city in more ways than one. While there is a definite European elite, mostly composed of ex-Nazis as near as I could make out, their one little modern section of town is surrounded by a throbbing populace of Indians much greater than in Quito or Lima in proportion to the elite population. The city is very hilly with the elite section in the center of a steep valley. In the distance is a very beautiful snow-capped mountain that dominates over the city. One minor observation I had is the city is stone crazy about advertisements for soft drinks. On one of the tallest buildings is a giant painting of an orange drink, on all the curbs one sees advertising for one drink or another; on buses, signs, everywhere one looks is a pop advertisement. "Pop art" is what I suppose it should be termed—ha ha.

La Paz is the last place we attempted to do any real business. I got all ready to go and Jerry didn't want to so I got mad at him. I later decided that the chance of making any money was so slim that it was not worth hassling with Jerry over. Anyway before I blew it off I did meet Fernando. We got to be great friends. He was quite excited at doing business with us, but he is young and I don't think anything will ever come of it. His mother-in-law told me of him when I went to the Embassy to inquire about any leads. We met the next day and he took Jerry and me out for lunch and was most congenial. He asked us if there was anything we wanted to do, and we said meet some girls, almost jokingly, but he took it quite seriously and a few days later after we met for lunch he took us to the fanciest whorehouse in town.

So we got to see another side of whoring in Latin America. These ladies were more beautiful and less trafficked than the Puno whores. They worked in a house in what passed for a middle-class neighborhood. We went in the middle of the day and had a good time with them. They did a striptease in the middle of a regularly furnished living room. I was attracted to one who looked like Ali McGraw. She told me that she'd come from the country to make money to support her daughter. I read between the lines and decided that someone had knocked her up, then cast her out. But that did not stop me from going into a regularly furnished bedroom with her. It was like they'd moved into a house that a family had left or maybe still used when not serving as a whorehouse.

Some may say rightly that whores are a perversion of the most basic of human needs, the need for love, touch and sex. I felt something for my "Ali" look-alike—even if for just a few hours. And I think that maybe she liked me a bit too. I do not object to them because they deal with so many men. They perform, I suppose, a much needed and sorely unattended function. And who can blame them if they don't appear to like their work? Of course it's not right to generalize or pontificate but my general impression when observing such goings on is that the women do not like their customers and do not like their jobs. Which I suppose could be said of women and men of all professions from sales lady to housewife. We are all whores in many ways, selling our souls and time in ways that betray our own natures. At least it can be said for these women that they tend to real basic needs in people—like nurses, but rather than honored they are paid well and made unrespectable.

After our visit to the whorehouse, Fernando took us home to meet his wife and child and take us to a party. He warned us to be sure not to mention anything to his wife. He had paid for us at the whorehouse, but had not utilized the sexual favors of the ladies. When we met his wife I understood why—she was beautiful.

Latin American men quite ordinarily have the wife and the kids and then a lady or ladies on the side. So many deceptions and false guises of respectability, it really is funny. The elites and their little trips. At the dance of Fernando's I didn't feel like dancing, though it was a good rumba band. This upset Fernando and he took me outside to find out what was wrong. I couldn't make him understand that I was just feeling mellow. Everyone, even down there, wants you to go crazy at a party or else they think you're having a bad time. Though we didn't know it at the time, we were showing bad manners by not actively participating.

We had met these people, one a girl Patty who I really liked and she me but she had her old man with her. One day we all took a bus out to Tiahuanaco, some ruins thirty miles from La Paz. These were my favorite ancient sites. Great stone slabs and ruins of buildings, plus erect statues stood on the outskirts of this small town with a cathedral. I sat there among the vestiges of the past and gazed out at the tremendous plateau of the Altiplano. It was the most quiet place I have ever been. It was as if one could hear a cricket chirp a mile off, but there were not even any crickets, not a sound disturbed the silence. Wind could be heard gathering twenty miles off and then it would rush around you and gust off trailing its lessening sound behind it as it disappeared. Little boys came up and sold us nice little clay figures for about a nickel. They were some of the best souvenirs I saw on the whole trip. One piece that I traded Patty's old man for is a genuine piece of art. The caretaker there claims to have dug it up. It certainly appears to be authentic but it's probably just soapstone. Whatever, it's the best souvenir I got on my trip including my poncho. I did do a lot of shopping around in La Paz and finally bought a nice Alpaca sweater for $10.

On the bus ride back from the ruins I became an inadvertent smuggler. We caught the last bus back to La Paz and it was jammed to the brink with people going to the market and for the big parade the next day. We all had to stand or rather crouch, the bus being too small to stand up in, and bounced on down the road. I asked some people if they would sell us their seats but then started feeling like the ugly American so I tried to hang loose and endure the ride. Much to their credit all the Indians had refused my money so I was most amazed when 15 minutes later a lady stood up and insisted that I take her seat. Well my chivalry prevailed and I refused saying that the lady standing with her baby should have it if anyone. This started a tremendous ruckus with the big bull goose mama of the lot demanding that I sit down immediately. Well that much convincing did the trick and with a conscious burdened with guilt I gladly sat down.

Her reason soon became apparent as we approached a checkpoint and guards boarded the bus and started going through the mounds of bundles stowed throughout. They were really quite brutal and thorough; taking what they wanted in the way of food and over the loud protest of the women began confiscating blankets right and left. It seems that we were in the midst of a great blanket bust. The ladies were transporting Peruvian blankets to the market without paying the duty. I had wondered why my seat was so uncommonly comfortable. I was sitting on a bunch of smuggled blankets!

As the cop approached I played it cool and sure enough he checked all those around me but let the gringo be. After we left the ladies loved me for helping them with their smuggling and kept patting me on the back and smiling at me and I had a comfortable trip home to La Paz.

Oro (the Spanish translation of Jerry's last name) and I had now been waiting for Klontz for over a week. We knew that even rushing he could not possibly reach us before the 12th of June. Gary had told me that paradise was to be found in a small village on the shores of Lago Titicaca called Sorata. We had talked to people who had just returned from there and were covered with those same nasty bites we had received in Peru. Needless to say I was loath to encounter those pesky little buggers again, but those people likewise confirmed that Sorata was indeed a beautiful spot. So we made preparations to go. Besides my llama-wool sweater, Bolivia had the nicest souvenirs—from llama-wool woven products to old coins and silver, to ancient weavings all for a bargain price. I had been unable to purchase much in Peru due to my financial state but did bring back quite a haul from La Paz. However I was unable to find a poncho I liked as much as the ones in Cuzco and finally had Jon buy me one on his way back north from Argentina.

After a final debate we decided to wait for Jon rather than go to Sorata and two days later he appeared at our door. He was exhausted from his hard journey but we on the other hand were raring to go. We took him out to our favorite restaurant where the beef was fantastic but as we were later to find out a mere foreshadowing of things to come in Argentina.

The next day we made travel arrangements and departed the following afternoon. It was necessary to make the first 150 kms by bus. To our surprise the road was paved and the bus comfortable. We arrived at the town only to discover that the train we intended to take was sold out in first class. We discussed taking second class but decided to spend the night in town and leave the following day. We saw a movie and walked home through the cold deserted streets. With few streetlights, clear air, and high altitude you can see the stars of the southern hemisphere very clearly.

The next day we boarded the train, a vintage model to say the least. It was good we had decided not to take second class though first class was not much better. We did have seats but the car was crammed wall to wall with people and their articles. As we waited to depart I was again amazed at the tremendous strength and endurance of the porters. Little men of common height for those parts, not more than 5'2" would bend over and using ropes strapped around their bodies and heads lift tremendous weights onto their backs and carry them off bent over almost double.

Finally we left, tacking out on a long bridge over this large lake and began the big haul to Buenos Aires. We had bought some wine and since our accommodations were so cramped, we grabbed the cards and went in search of a comfortable place to drink and play. Lounge cars are not to be found in Bolivian trains and the nearest we could find was the dining facility, by far the nicest car on the train. We sat ourselves down and ordered a beer and two glasses and told them we would also like to drink our wine there. As you can imagine the idea of us camping out with our own stash was not eagerly embraced by the establishment.

Jon went back to have the first of many talks with the maitre-d', laid a little money on him and we were allowed to drink our wine. But then after we broke out the cards, the owner of the car, it being a private enterprise, informed us that we must buy something or leave. So I bought some lunch—a horrible tough piece of pork if I recall correctly and managed to stay in there for an hour or more, but finally had to retire to our cramped quarters in the rear, which if you can believe it had become even more crowded. There was not even room to walk down the aisle. After an hour of that we decided it was time for dinner and again sojourned up to the dining car.

As one might imagine the dining car establishment was not overjoyed to see us. Well, I thought, our money is good, and these military chaps have been camped out in the back of the car the whole trip. We were told that dinner was not to be served for another hour and we could not wait. They would not even serve us a drink saying that we were "malcriado"— poorly raised.

Such nonsense. But we took it well enough and again returned to our car which if you can again stretch your imagination had grown even more crowded—packed to the brim, bursting at the seams. People and gear stuffed into every nook and cranny. It would not be unfair to say that we were rather unpopular at this end too, since upon returning others were forced out of our most desired seats and into the already cramped aisle.

After an hour or two here we genuinely became hungry and mustering our forces we marched again to the dining car where we were told all the tables had been reserved for a girls' school. God knows where a girls' school was going to appear from in the vast uninhabited wastelands that were speeding by our window. Well I thought enough of this bull-ul-ll shit and in my best form demanded that Jon have harsh words with the establishment.

J.K. to say the least is not the harshest person and managed only to inquire if the military had some special prerogative since the two of them were still bivouacked in the car. That to say the least was a naïve question.

"The military run the country," he was told, "and may do whatever they like."

So I sat down and became the first American-Bolivian freedom rider. I again asked to be served and again was called "malcriado."

It soon looked as if we were going to get the boot and the situation was growing dire.

Jon Klontz is such a totally laid back and naturally modest person that I was genuinely surprised when upon urging from Jerry and me, he pulled out this old defunct diplomatic passport he had from when he was living with his father who is a State Department doctor and presented it to the "jefe" of the dining car.

This created something more than a mild stir but we still were not getting the grub and it wasn't until two military cats chipped in on our behalf that we finally got served. We ended up striking up an acquaintance with these guys and stayed in the car until late in the night drinking and playing a dice game. By the way, the girls' school or a bunch of girls did appear and my how they fussed over the lieutenants.

Being in the army (down there) is about the most common way to get ahead and if you get any rank you've got it made unless of course you end up on the wrong side of a revolution.

We did in fact witness a bit of a revolt. One night in La Paz tanks and stuff came rolling down the street. And Jerry saw some students get gassed at the university once. Before Banzer (General Hugo Banzer, President of Bolivia) the present ruling general, there was trouble at the same university and they strafed and bombed it. This time some dissenters got creamed in Cochabamba but the next day we saw Banzer walking in this parade.

It was cold and grey so we didn't stay for the whole thing. What it was is every year each section of the city has its own affair and this one was by the market area and a hot one. Hundreds of people in fantastic devil gargoyle, bear and even American Indian costumes; amazing costumes and masks—all dancing and whirling around and up and down the street—it was the most colorful and vibrant parade I had ever seen.

But anyway, there we were with army cats on the train and we had some interesting conversations that night as we got high on beer and playing those games. One particular idea they had was that Bolivia was the hub of the universe and all was well and prosperous, which it was for them.

We argued that we had just read that there was near famine in Bolivia.

"Hunger!" They retorted, "look at the food you ate tonight."

Yeah we had eaten well and so had the other elites. For them the fact that Indians starve is meaningless. They might as well be from another time, much less living in the same country with groups of people supposed to be sharing their national and economic destiny. One of the greatest economic problems of South America, particularly the Andean states, is a feeling that there is us and them and there is a complete ignorance among the elites that their future well-being is directly connected to the Indians. That is, if they continue to exploit the Indians and take the profits out of the country rather than reinvest them in educating the people and developing the land, their countries will go on in a perpetual cycle of poverty with them having to live in it. Nobody wants to live in a slum.

Fernando, after showing us the nice residential part of La Paz, said that the really rich people move to Miami Beach and it is a cliché how the rulers in the country steal what they can and put it in Swiss banks, never to be seen in their own economy. What isn't stolen is invested in military equipment to supply the army. If one has cash to invest on the side one puts it into the American-European market.

The U.S. is right in the middle of this. They sell the arms to the military, house and educate the rich. But the U.S. is not to be completely faulted, whatever development there is in these countries owes a lot to U.S. investment in equipment and education. Labor of course costs next to nothing. The resulting cycle is one where money pours through these countries like a sieve and there is little effort to halt it or create national capital of their own. My god, any of these countries has the resources to develop tremendous industries of their own.

I have to admire the progressive military in Peru, which is telling outside interests, all right there is copper there but it's going to stay there until we can develop the industry ourselves by our own means. That is not to say that Peru does not have a vested interest and is not trapped in the same "under development" cycle, but there is at least a glimmering of notion that the most valuable resource is the people, and if they are properly cared for, invested in, and "developed"; i.e., educated and fed properly so that they might obtain their intellectual potential, all will eventually prosper and be the better for it.

Today in Peru one sees cooperatives all over the countryside. While I heard that they are not working any economic miracles the cooperatives are indicative of a positive intervention on the part of the government; an investment in the people. On the other hand I should note that the present regime also recently cracked down on the free press and Lima is surrounded by shantytowns—"barrios." The education I witnessed in Cuzco was militaristic with the children lined up in uniforms, rank and file, singing some national hymn.

Anyway, back on the train we finally got kicked out of that very comfortable diner and went back to our own car to try and sleep, and by god if that place was not fit to explode with people and gear filled to the absolute brim with people and things. Our entrance was the straw, as they say. The joint exploded with groans and crying babies and just as it seemed as if we were all doomed to be scattered all over the arid salt flats of middle Bolivia the train stopped at a seemingly innocuous enough place and lo, half the train piled off. The relief, divine intervention, suddenly there was all this room. Well not to pass up a good space, I had learned my lessons well by this point and was soon bedded down as comfortably as might be expected. The night was not all peace and beauty but I managed a bit of sleep.

In the morning we found ourselves out of the Altiplano and into this desert area, reminiscent of Arizona with wind and rock sculptures and arid beauty of brown sand and red rock.

We arrived in the middle of the day at the Argentine border. Being Sunday we had to wait until the proper border authority showed up. Jon and Jerry went to look for him and I stayed and waited, jiving with the guards and playing music. The town itself was silent and burning in the hollow desert mountain air. The official showed up and after a mad dash through the town I couldn't find the boys so the guy decided to leave. At the last minute we all got together and left Bolivia.

Entering into Argentina was a revelation. No border I have ever crossed was as radically different, with the possible exception of San Diego—Tijuana. The Bolivian side was dusty streets, adobe houses, small stores with poor stock, and Indians. The Argentina side was paved streets, European cars, "smart" well-stocked shops full of appliances and conveniences. The resulting impression from the contrast of the two towns led me to reinforce a predisposition that the Caucasian communities of this world have got something going for them economically. Argentina has been in decline economically for the past 20 years. They have the resources to be one of the richest and most beautiful countries in the world. At the moment they have no government worth a damn and the social order is in complete chaos. Argentina was my favorite country in many ways and I'll always be fond of it.

We got our passports stamped after a delay (never cross borders on Sunday if possible), and bought tickets for an all night trip to

Hippies camping in Pereyra Irola with infamous snail and bamboo pot pipe.

Tucumán. After seeing half of the French Connection and some other film about running from something we started again on the long road to Buenos Aires. All that night we traveled with the hours and miles blurring. The bus and road were modern and comfort seemed amazing compared to what we were used to.

Jon and I had a quick but interesting conversation on the first night on the bus. He was quite pensive and I asked of his mood. At first I thought he was saddened by the fact his father has cancer and I thought I could help by telling how long my father survived with his illness. But no, he was thinking about politics, it turned out later. Having lived in and studied South America very closely, Jon is down on the present structure and sees no hope without revolution of change; i.e., "the only true revolution was in Cuba." He does not count coups where the next government again plays right into the hands of the elites and the U.S. government. Jon wants to help with money but being a peaceful sort can't see himself getting out there and fighting.

The night passed and the next day cities such as Jujay, Salta, were only stops.

Argentina

In the morning of our first day in Argentina the bus arrived in Salta and we had a few hours until the bus left for Cordoba. Jon, as I have said, knows much of South America. We had asked him if gauchos still existed in Argentina, and he correctly informed us that while they still existed in small numbers, by and large, they were a myth of folklore. So he was in for quite a good deal of embarrassment when upon leaving the bus station we found gauchos dressed in their finest garb and fanciest horses riding up and down the streets. At first we thought it funny, then curious when we came upon more and more. As it turned out there was a parade that morning to honor some military hero. On the way to the ceremonies we passed the parade forming and after eating from vendors we saw them pass in review with tanks but mostly mounted gauchos and police.

At the reviewing site was all this brass. Jerry and Jon bet me ten dollars to streak across the plaza in front of the generals. The idea was appealing enough except for the drawback that I would most likely be shot on the spot and if captured probably locked up and deported back to the U.S. But oh the publicity. I might have made "Time."

That noon we had our first meal in a restaurant. The food in

Argentina is the best I've eaten in the world. With great Italian influence, fantastic wines, very cheap, the lowest dive will provide one with a delicious fare and a timely repast. Wine with every meal, oh, lordy, that Argentinian food. We walked around Salta some more. It seemed every time we turned the corner we'd run into that darn horse parade.

It felt odd to be at something resembling sea level. After months in the high Andes a walk of a mile or two seemed comparatively effortless.

There was a train from Salta to Buenos Aires but it was more expensive and took longer than the bus. So that afternoon we boarded a bus to Córdoba got there early the next morning and immediately boarded another bus for Buenos Aires. By now the hours just rolled by as did the wide spaces of the Pampas. I slept a lot and made the mistake perhaps prompted by thoughts of Felipe (Felipe Jolly-Luque, a friend of Jon and mine from the American International School of Vienna) of "flicking" on Jon. That vilest of habits whereby one places a bit of churned up saliva on the tip of the index finger and flicks it onto a target—usually the body of a good friend. To do it on anyone else would more than likely lead to bloodshed. Jerry loved it and joined right in. Jon got right back into his Mr. Innocent role. As he would flick or instigate a flick and then say "okay, stop, stop, you started it!" Flick—"okay that's the end no more—truce." Always after he got the last flick in. We almost got in real trouble by fighting around some of the Argentine National Rugby Team, but they got to be friends with us and one showed us how to get to Felipe's.

After days on the plains we were drawing closer to Buenos Aires and I was ready for it too. Ready to kick back for a week or two and ready to see Felipe. We thought we might make it by evening, but the bus broke down and it was nine o'clock before we hit the outskirts of Buenos Aires. God! Superhighways even.

We got off the bus finally. Took a cab and then the rapid transit for one stop and were in Acassuso. We had tried to call from where the bus had broken down but were unable to get through. So it was a complete surprise to Mrs. Jolly (Felipe's mother) when Jon rang the buzzer at her apartment building. "Si" "Mrs. Jolly?" "Yes?" "This is Jon Klontz." "You're kidding!" "And Jeff Oshins." "My God! Come up!"

What a welcome—more than we ever hoped for. "Come in, come in. Felipe's not here, out playing with his band." Records, stereo, rugs, modern apartment. Great view. After months in the wilderness, it seemed like the ultimate in luxury. Our first home-cooked meal in ages. Steaks. Argentine steaks. Mrs. Jolly said she would turn the apartment over to us and go to her mother's. Finally I went to sleep. But only for a moment and Jolly comes in.

He, Jon, and I had traveled around California in my VW bug and had taken a trip down to Baja, Mexico a couple of years before, but Felipe never thought I'd make it to Buenos Aires. He expected Jon sometime in the future but never me too. What a reunion! I felt warm and welcome. But I also felt tired so after long hugs and much celebration, while Jon, Jerry and Felipe talked the night away, I slept.

In the morning, Felipe had to go to work so we all tagged along for our first trip to the big city. I wanted to pick up some funds at the Bank of America but mostly we all just tripped around the fine spacious boulevards of Buenos Aires. A beautiful city and easily compared with Paris. There was nothing for me at the bank and wasn't to be for many weeks, but the days slipped by with good times and beautiful women. The women down there are almost as fun as the wine, but much fancier. Great dressers, high fashion is very hip and the women deserve it. Those long Italian legs and Argentine-Spanish eyes. Mama Mia!

Felipe took me to a party at some friends—very cosmopolitan European types. And I sat down and in came this beautiful girl and walks right up to me and kisses me on the cheek—"Well, honey," I thought, "You've obviously got good taste." But then she continued around the room kissing everyone else—quaint custom if I do say so myself. I played some tunes for them and we all got along fine.

Felipe's apartment was all ours now. His mother acted as a fairy godmother bringing us over food every day or so but mostly just leaving us to ourselves. The apartment was on the 13th floor of a high-rise over the hippodrome or race track and bounded on the other side by the La Plata River. Tremendous view.

The horses remind me of one of my first experiences in Quito. Oro and I went to this dumpy track where the same old nags ran time and again so they would give them drugs right in front of everyone and what you would bet on was which horse had gotten the best fix that day. I didn't know that and bet on the first race. There was this giant in the field of small horses—a real strider from his looks named—Aquardiente—firewater. He seemed unbeatable by the competition but got wiped by this little pony with about

100 cc of cocaine running through his veins—brr-rooom. The horses of Argentina were slick and sophisticated in comparison to the others we had seen, as was everything else. Being in Argentina was like coming back to the twentieth century and I was not sorry to have that interlude. Read books, listened to records, ate steaks, played music, dated these lovely high steppin' Argentina women. Ah lovely. Two weeks slipped by quite fast and one day we all set out for the country.

Felipe thought he knew a park we could camp at. We found ourselves then on a country lane goofing around the elms, taking pictures, asking of this place. It was closed or didn't exist but Felipe talked to the manager of this great country estate who gave us permission to camp out on the grounds. What a place, surrounding the castle or whatever were parks and woods all for ourselves.

Felipe took a bunch of pictures of us mostly centering around the great bong—that being a pipe created to be used in inhaling a bit of the old weed. And a magical device it was too. Created with ingenuity from found objects—bamboo, a snail shell, and a discarded bit of cloth and aluminum.

The scene was wide and comfortable. We all ran up and over the trees, verily elves we were in the leaves. We were rained upon that night but had tents up and it was only drizzle and what the hell.

We set out for La Plata, got rained on, saw a movie, decided to go back to Felipe's country estanzia the other side of Buenos Aires. We tripped upon a really first rate dinosaur bone museum. We decided to go back late at night rather than get a room. So after the movie we were waiting around, had a good meal. Felipe had this monster portion of meat called "baby beef" —a hunk of filet that would scare a roast beef off the rack.

Afterwards we walked past this discotheque and though we didn't go in we were the smash attraction. Crowds gathered around us as the word spread that Americans were outside. The kids down there are surrounded by increments of the U.S. but not many of them had ever seen in the flesh that which they had heard and seen so much about in movies and songs.

The much heralded American hippie. A couple of the "hippist" Argentines tried to collar us for status or something. We each had our own little group. One chick took Jerry inside and next we saw him kissing her on the patio. The scene began to break up and the cats who were trying to collar us finally got us together to go to some bar which turned out to be a drag. I danced with the only girl there as did everyone else. We then wandered through the late rain-soaked streets of La Plata and ended up at this whore bar where we, or I should say, I led this little floozy on for a few minutes. Meanwhile everyone else was conking out except our guides who couldn't seem to get enough of us.

Again we were confronted with, as are many Americans, the superfluous hospitality factor, being our cold alienated selves such outpourings of instant devotion put us back a bit and besides somehow we always ended up paying for their drinks. Dirty conniving spics—ha —we were onto their game.

We finally boarded a bus about 4:30 a.m. and tootled on back to Buenos Aires.

We stopped off at the apartment, picked up the car and some

food and headed out again. Driving in Buenos Aires is in a word insane. Macho gone wild. Like it's a mortal insult if someone passes you. And then there are these cops, Nazgûls, flying around with guns and checkpoints and outriggers on their bikes.

We pulled into Felipe's country house and I crashed out. That night we went into town and created just about the same scene at the local discotheque there. Even ol' Jon got off on it, playing old Beatles and dancing with all those lovely, hungry Argentine women.

Jon and Jerry went home but Felipe and I went back and chatted it up a bit more with the ladies.

The next morning Argentina was playing in the semifinals of the World Cup and the town was in an uproar. Unfortunately or perhaps fatefully, we were observed by the groundskeeper of Felipe's place to be kicking a ball around in a soccer-like manner, no matter that it was a tennis ball. Whatever it was, I pulled a muscle in my side doing it.

Welp, we were presently inquired of by the groundskeeper if we would care to participate in a small soccer game that afternoon. I had nothing to say about the matter but didn't think it that big a deal. Well, we watched the game and I was sort of into it—soccer that is. Argentina lost the game so we went back to whatever we were doing—reading, I believe, when the all but forgotten groundskeeper came over inquiring if we were ready to go play *fútbol*.

So off we went to the field and, goddamn, if the whole town hadn't turned out for the event. Little kids hanging out of trees, girls packed three deep along the side lines, and all the hyped up machos in town whooping and hollering.

I asked what was happening here and was told that this was where we were going to play. It seems we were to be on the team of other foreigners. Like the whole town figured they were going to have their own World Cup right there. And I tell you, the scene could not have been any less intense if we were in Munich playing the final game of the Cup.

Felipe and Jon had been on our high school soccer team in Vienna, which wasn't such a bad team. Jon was even on the varsity at American University, got All American or Most Valuable Player or something. Jerry had also played a bit in college but ol' J.O. didn't know a soccer ball from the man on the moon.

Somehow I was assigned the position of goalie. Well, the opposition scored some quick ones. As it turned out I was not positioning myself properly giving them too wide an angle to shoot at. Jon gave me some quick advice and I started to make some saves, all which caused the crowd to boo and the kids sitting above me in the tree to throw mud—not at me but near enough to arouse my suspicion that they were attempting to distract the goalie from his assigned task of stopping goals. With a bit of advice from Jon on proper positioning I managed to stop a few goals. Like the time this cat wound up the old boot and let it fly from about two feet in front of me that caught me up the side of my head. The crowd loved it and thought it was the greatest save they had ever seen and I immediately became a star of sorts (though at the time the only stars I was concerned with were the ones I was seeing in my head). I have never had my bell rung like that before and hope if I studiously avoid ever playing soccer again, I will avoid having it rung in like manner again.

My heroics seemed to inspire the team and Jerry scored a goal of all things. But I never once thought we were going to win. But then something odd began to happen. I can only say that beginners' luck or some divine intervention took place.

A similar occurrence had taken place in La Paz to Jerry and me. While waiting for Jon we met these three cats who had been with a British expedition to the South Pole for two years and had spent the time almost entirely devoting themselves to playing bridge with each other. Well to say they knew each other's games and how to interpret bids would be a colossal understatement. They were hot and just killing us when suddenly fate intervened and between us, for the next seven hands, Jerry and I never had less than 10 of the cards of the same suit. These cats couldn't believe us when we kept bidding 7's and 6's and kept thinking we were bluffing, whereby they would double and redouble.

Well, we socked it good to those limeys and don't you know, we started putting it to the Argentine "National" team (or so they thought themselves). They were actually a rag-taggle batch of butchers and farmers. There were a few hotshots, but toward the end we seemed to be in better shape. And then the fast break was introduced to soccer in Argentina.

Me and this Chilean dude teamed up like this. I would get the ball down at my end of the field. Now the proper method of putting a ball back in play was to roll or throw it out and then both teams would battle it out up to the other end of the field. So while most of the opposition was at my end of the field, I would then put a lot of hiking boot into the ball and get it down to this fellow who then would be one-on-one and always then would score a goal (OK—anyone who knows sqaut about soccer is now correctly observing that we were probably offside, and truth there were no ref's in this game. We played and nobody said anything.) So we quickly started racking up goals and finally won by one point. It wasn't Canadian Club but we bought beer and had a hearty congratulations from the team and the town. That night we went back to Buenos Aires. I, muddy-faced, bruised and resolved to stay way from that game if at all possible in the future.

Mrs. Jolly Luque was to leave in a week for Venezuela where she was coming out of retirement to lend her considerable editing and translating skills to the cause of the United Nations Conference on the Law of the Seas. Though her hospitality was boundless, it was obvious that she would rather we be gone when she left. She seemed to be wanting Felipe to get back to his orderly life. That being composed mainly of his job (English lessons), his girlfriend Claire, a pretty petite of British lineage who pretty well had ol' Felipe in hand. Felipe and I discussed it later and though he certainly appeared to and went through all the motions, we decided it was a classic case of a disease to which we both are terribly susceptible and had suffered many times on account of the inability to feel the old wham zing full kind of head-over-heels number with a girl that feels the same way about you. As we put it "we only fall in love with those that don't love us."

Mrs. Jolly's departure was to take place at the end of our third week in Buenos Aires so the timing was fine for us. Except that the Bank of America had not come up with my money. As the day approached for our departure I was not certain that I would be leaving.

On the day before we were going to leave, Jerry and I went to the Embassy to take what turned out to be a final and futile stab at doing some business. While talking to the commercial consul, we heard from him that Perón, the fabulous political figure of the century and the only man who could hold the diversified Argentine political factions together was sick and perhaps dead. A few hours later we read on a newsboard in the middle of the city that Perón was dead.

Everything immediately shut down and I quite expected to see people weeping on the streets, but saw nothing like it. Nothing like the weeping scenes of the day Roosevelt died. We all went back to the suburbs, to the apartment where we waited, not knowing what to expect. Argentina is a very volatile place. One hears more than one sees of violence. I saw practically no violence, whereas Gary and Marsea saw a man shot in Colombia and we read constantly in the newspaper of political assassinations and had heard tales of riots and violent clashes between right and left wing peronisti.

Somehow Perón had managed to return from exile in Spain. An old man, a once-deposed Nazi sympathizer, wartime leader returns and both the right and left claimed him for their own with labor feeling a special kinship. When he ruled during and after World War II, Perón had managed to do quite well by labor, but in the meantime, Argentina had slipped from being one of the world's richest countries to just hanging on. Upon his return, Perón rode in on a wave of popular approval that was truly gigantic. But he was old and the forces who sought his leadership were too diversified and too much and often at each other's throats to be led anywhere by anyone.

There is no reason for Argentina to be lacking anything. Even without reaching their production potential they export wheat and beef. The country has a tremendous coastline and yet I was told by the U.S. Commercial Consulate that the country had almost no fishing industry. We saw plains and plains of fertile land that really rivals the midwest (U.S. midwest) in size. Yet due to either poor production techniques or export practices, food was being rationed with beefless months, beef being the main export commodity. I would deduce that it was due more than likely to the need to have a commodity to trade for manufactured products. Often Latin American countries will trade off so much of their main crop that the people will suffer shortages.

Particularly poignant were people who had planted and harvested bean crops in Central America having to stand in lines or pay inflated prices for this, the staple of their diet, on account of so much of it being traded to U.S. and Europe so that the elites can buy cars and appliances in western markets or worse, guns and weapons in those markets.

As I have already noted, Argentina is rich compared to its northern neighbors. There are modern agricultural tools, roads, good transportation and communications systems and good social mobility among its Euro-stock population. There are little or no Indians left.

The next day I was forced to impose on Mrs. Jolly to extend her hospitality a week or two longer as my money had not come and was nowhere in sight. Jon and Jerry were packing. I broached the point with a bit of trepidation but Mrs. Jolly, seeing that the other two were on their way out, and reassured by me that I would find a place to stay while she was packing up, consented that I could stay a while longer.

That night we took Jon and Jerry to the train. Quite a difference between its comfortable seats, bathing lavatory and that bumpy piece of funk we rode through Bolivia. As the three of us stood there with Felipe, knowing that though the three of us would soon meet up again, the camaraderie was broken. Argentina would soon be over for Jon and Jerry.

Jerry went out in style though. There was this beautiful classic Argentina filly getting on the train. We joked about it. Felipe teasing Jon that Jerry would be giving him some competition. As it turned out Jerry and Jon met this other chick that they kept trying to get rid of all the way through Argentina and Bolivia. The second day on the train Jerry and Jon and the grosso sex fiend California school teacher were hanging out in the back of the train and Jerry, as he tells it, decided to mosey back to his seat, as apparently Linda, the blonde California lady was looking for some good ol' kinky California sex and trying to interest Hermie as Jerry was referred to by this hog. She must have been really bad because Jerry demurred.

Jerry sat down in his seat and the beautiful Argentine girl walked by and the eyes met, a little talk, then the hands and in five minutes they were locked in the old embrace. Linda and Jon walked back and to hear it, Linda apparently just about lost it upon seeing Jerry, so soon after he'd wandered off, in the arms of a beautiful Argentine girl. Needless to say Jerry had a nice train trip. Even though both he and the girl had decided they loved each other—love at first sight—the girl got off in Córdoba or Jujay (someplace like that) a few hours after they had "met."

Poor Jon was stuck with Linda. When they got to the border late at night, they could only find two beds—one double and a single. It turned out to be a joke because Jerry the rat took the single and Jon came home from some drinking to find ol' Linda waiting for him. Jon managed to retain his honor and apparently Linda never forgave him. According to Jon, demon alcohol saved him as he passed out! And though Jon , like myself, is not exactly in a position of having to bat the willing girls back, he has never had a moment's regret. Linda traveled on with them and wanted to go with Jon to Cuzco. The boys managed to ditch her in La Paz, or perhaps it was Cochabamba. Whatever, we soon were all going our own way.

After Felipe, Ladybug (his girlfriend), and I left Jon and Jerry off at the train we got robbed and at the most expensive or at least most luxurious hotel in town. We had walked all over town looking for a place to eat, but could not find a place that wasn't closed on account of Perón's death, except this fancy-dansy hotel. Well, I said I never had a bad meal in Argentina, but this came pretty close. A choice between fish and chicken, including dessert. We were not even seated in the main dining room but rather out in a foyer. I also had a beer. We figured the price might be a bit steep, but were shocked at the bill—$30— ten smackers per—worse meal in

Argentina and likewise service. For Argentina that was the equivalent of a week's fine, fine eating. Well I just laughed and said, we should pay half and if they didn't like it we would just hotfoot it—which wasn't a good idea really since the place was crawling with police. Two Japanese guests were flipping out too. Felipe just argued with the guy claiming we never got dessert. Since the restaurant had let the Asians go for half, they finally let us off for $15 which was still highway robbery.

We paid and split. Felipe was mad at himself because he had gotten mad at the maître d'. Whatever he said, did the trick through, with the maître d' telling Felipe not to threaten him. Felipe was just having one of his occasional attacks of "I ain't no good blues." Too bad to see him like that. So we walked home through the streets and I talked to him of appreciating the beauty of the moment and seeing the positive aspects of just being alive. I guess where I see a friend blue for no other reason than some head trip they're on I have to come on with the philosophy which comes down to good ol' be-here-now, keep your mind open to the moment. Being and nothingness—*L'Être et le néant*—just turn those bad thoughts off because they are going to help no one solve anything. Don't bring yourself down—just be.

As I recall I also gave him a bit of the old "you have to know down to know when you're up." I personally endure the downs because I like the ups and prefer the up and down to being always in the middle in some grey glowing cloud of anxiety in which I see most people existing. Stumbling through life waiting for some blast to knock them out of their dreary daze and into some spot where they are ecstatic orgasmic every second, feeling like they don't ever want to leave, conscious of everything that is transpiring around them. Those moments are the spice of life for me but even if I am down I try to be aware of why I am down and feel the down. Feel it, be conscious of my body, so much better than all the zombies I see on the street stumbling along chewing their lips, their hands clenched, just bummed, not even aware of it, they're so twisted in knots. Dig the moment if it's up or down—be there wherever it is.

Our philosophical pattering was stopped and our minds zipped back to the moment by a most amazing sight of at least a hundred thousand, maybe much more, people eight abreast. A line stretching for blocks and blocks perhaps 30 in all. I have never seen so many people in one place, all lined up to pass for a second's glance in front of the body of Perón. Which apparently started to bleed around the gills now and then. On TV there was a nurse standing there to mop up the corpse.

There was a crowd of elite who got to stop behind the corpse for a short period as the masses, some having stood for more than a day, passed for a quick glance of "el patrón".

His wife, now the president, struck the old stiff upper lip. But damn, what a job she has—she's still at it. Started out with Perón when he was hanging out in Panamá. The disposed dictator roaming the world. He ended up in Spain with the cabaret dancer who is now the head of state of one of the most politically explosive, yet economically promising, countries in the world. Plus Perón's old wife is a saint—Saint Eva. A hard act to follow. The Patron Saint of the Unions, working class mama. There are still whole Argentine societies dedicated to carrying out her legacy. Good luck, Isabella.

The following day I moved out of Felipe's into a friend of his. I thought I was being friendly. I helped them sand a floor they were working on and went up to my room where I practiced my music and experimented with recording a few songs I had written. Something I did however, I think it was being friendly to the cat's girlfriend, ticked them off and Felipe came by and we split. Very strange. So then I moved into a boarding house where Felipe's American girlfriend had stayed. I had an enjoyable stay for five days or so and moved back to Felipe's after his mama left.

We had a good time playing music and reading. I became addicted to P.G. Wodehouse and read about a book a day. I stayed another week and finally after much hassling, got the BofA to wire for my money. Then there was a period of delay because they did not have any dollars. There is a thriving quasi-legitimate black market where you can get 1 and 2/3 for your dollar. Like the official rate is about 9 pesos to the dollar and the blackmarket rate is 15.

I finally settled for travelers' checks and the bank gave them to me for free since I had been waiting for so long. I then took the money over to a travel agency and changed about a hundred into cash, bought a plane ticket to Quito, and was all set.

The last night I was there I took Felipe and Claire to the fanciest place in town where we did have an incomparable beef dinner. Just amazing. It cost me about $25 but would have been $40 according to the official rate. I love black markets. They are dangerous enough to make things exciting and you always feel as if you're getting some fantastic deal.

Like when I was in Czechoslovakia, I spent a week trying to figure out the system. It seemed that you could easily find people who would change western currency at up to 8 times the official rate. The rule however was that on your visa you had to show that you had changed $4/day at the official rate. As it turned out I bought a leather jacket that has served me well for six years and is still going strong. The reason people were so anxious to exchange exorbitant amounts of Czech currency for $ was that western products could only be bought with western money at western stores. Like people offered me outrageous amounts of money for my jeans.

Five years later in Argentina, the government was again responsible through their policies of making it hard to get western currency at the banks for their citizens for a concurrent supply/demand market. This is a quite interesting phenomenon throughout the world which, though confusing, is often a bonus for western travelers.

Smugglers

I only had a week left until I was to meet Jerry and Jon in Quito and wanted to see some more of Argentina, so after a sad farewell I flew to a town called Mendoza which is in a valley close to the eastern slope of the Argentine Andes. I arrived in Mendoza and found the town humming with *turistas*. Some national holiday and had a hard time finding a place to stay.

I finally ended up at a small family pensión. I decided not to spend the three days I had allotted for Mendoza solely in the town. I found a bus up to the mountain, awoke at 5 a.m. and went to the station. While waiting there in the darkened platform, this fellow pulled up in a taxi loaded down with all kinds of gear, including some skis. We struck up a conversation about skiing in the Argentine mountains. His name was Nesel. He was an Argentine who worked at the world famous ski resort in Chile on the other side of the crest, Portillo.

He informed me that he intended to transport all this gear with aid of friends over the pass.

As we drove through the dawn up into the mountains, I became determined to accompany him and he was more than willing to have the extra help. What follows was the most adventurous two days of the trip.

By midday we had journeyed as far as the road was open and

were quite high in the mountains. The last town had been Punta de Vacas and we were deposited in this army camp. Nesel had gone off to arrange for some help in transporting his gear through the first leg of the trek. As I sat there in the midst of the high Andes I started to feel the effect of the extremely high altitude. While in Peru and La Paz I had grown acclimated to rarefied air and was able to climb and run about without pain. But my time in Buenos Aires had left me readjusted to sea-level, so while I was sitting there I began to have my doubts about going off into this snow-bound waste so ill-prepared. But the mountains looked so magnificent and Nesel seemed so confident that I decided I would go ahead with the expedition. Just then Nesel returned and informed me that the soldiers who were to have helped us had already left early that morning for maneuvers. So for the first of many times I wrongly assumed that "that was that." But Nesel was an extremely determined fellow. He went off and returned an hour later. He had arranged for us to ride this diesel engine 5 kms to the end of the track where we were to be met by some friends of his who would help us carry his gear to Los Cuevas, where we would spend the night.

By the time we got to the end of the track it was almost nightfall and his friends were nowhere in sight. We waited on the side of the tracks for Nesel's friends to show. As the sun went down the temperature dropped quickly. I had on every bit of clothing I had and was still freezing and it was getting colder.

Nesel broke out some of his extra gear; a sweater or two, a down vest and a down face mask. The problem was sitting around and not doing anything or moving.

At nightfall we started moving the gear into a workman's shack, planning to push on with what we could carry. I was still feeling the puna. This old man who lived up there in the snow waste gave us some mate de coca, an herb (coca) tea that was crammed into a special jar, hot water was poured on it, with a bit of sugar and a metal straw thrust into the mixture whereby one sucked and got this remarkable medicinal brew. It tasted branchy but did a fine job on my altitude sickness.

Just as we were preparing to take off, Nesel's friends came tromping down out of the mountains. Five huskier chaps I've never seen. Veritable mountain men they were.

Nesel said it was five miles ahead to where we were going and that I should follow the tracks. So I started out ahead while the rest loaded up, knowing that I would need the head start because I would have to rest along the way.

I struck out over this ice flow. There was only a quarter moon but everything seemed to glow and the stars seemed so numerous that they made the sky glow about the same as the snow. It was like another medium, another environment that I had never experienced before. It was silent and foreboding with shrill wind blowing off the sides of the mountain range and through the passes and across the flow.

I was carrying about 60 lbs on my back plus Nesel's skis and my guitar strapped on top, so the load was quite cumbersome and top heavy. I was fine as long as I stayed near the tracks because the ground was firmly covered and packed with snow and ice. However the tracks were hard to follow and all too often I would stray into the side and sink to my knees in snow or even to my waist, necessitating great effort to remove myself.

On one occasion the tracks led over a bridge and I put a step forward and was suddenly hanging in space over this gorge. That freaked me out and I stayed put until the rest arrived with the flashlights.

I had understood from Nesel that where we were headed was just through this tunnel up ahead. I kept plugging on thinking once we reached the tunnel looming on a big curve on the side of the mountain at the end of the flow that we would be just about there.

The tunnel was pitch black but sheltered us from the wind and with the flashlights and the evenly spaced railroad ties we could make good time in some spots, but then there were places where the metal covering had given in under the tremendous weight of the snow. At these avalanches I was at a tremendous disadvantage on account of the skis strapped across the top of my pack. Often there was only a small space that could be crawled through. At these times I would have to take everything off and push it through the break or over the mound and crawl after it.

We came out of the tunnel and I was startled by the stars. A clearer, more pollution-free, higher proximity to the heavens is rarely afforded a man.

As the hours and miles passed I became more tired. It became a great extra burden to have to stop and take my pack off, crawl around over a drift and go on. When we came to this one avalanche toward the end of the hike, the way was almost completely blocked.

By this time, the party had become strung out. I was with the lead group. I was about ready to throw it in and camp out there. Throw out the sleeping bag and hope that I didn't freeze. But the others, more experienced, insisted we go on.

We found a way over the top of the avalanche and crawled outside into the starry night and the winds. We walked on another mile, entered another tunnel and emerged at Las Cuevos, the caves. The last town in Argentina was completely buried under snow: cars, houses, everything. But I was never happier to see a town. I would have preferred to camp outside in the beautiful mountains but I was ready to stop.

We walked through a tunnel dug down to the door of the hotel where the mountain men were wintering it. To their great amusement I completely collapsed into a couch by the fire and began the long process of thawing out. I ate some soup and went right to bed.

In the morning we walked to the summit through a rock tunnel. The tunnel was easy going and full of ice flows and stalactites that hung from the roof. The tunnel was about 5 kms long and about half way through Nesel pointed his flashlight to the wall at the sign of the border between Argentina and Chile.

Nesel said that I should be proud or feel unique or something "very few people have ever seen what you have." True enough, but the best of the walk was yet to come.

When we emerged from the tunnel, Nesel took his skis, told me to follow his tracks, and skied on down to Portello. I set out in the cold brilliance more alone and closer to nature than I have ever been. It was midday and in the silence I could hear water trickling in the distance.

I hoisted my pack that much lighter and started the walk down. It was a rare moment and I appreciated every second of it, allowing my mind to bathe in every detail. I walked on and down the valley. As the valley broadened I saw in the distance among the jagged peaks a horn very similar to the Matterhorn. I had seen the Andes from jungle to desert tops but never was I so infinitely in touch with it as on these snowy reaches.

I walked the rest of the day. Still having trouble with soft snow traps. Occasionally I would stop and just vibrate in the clean silent air.

By nightfall as I approached the hotel I was tired but extremely high and blissful. Through the final tunnel I was sorry to be leaving my snowy solitude but was comforted with the thought of a hot bath and meal and some skiing the next day.

I had asked Nesel about the problem of not having a visa and he had assured me that I could get one at the hotel. While it was possible to maintain a checkpoint in Argentina, Chile had nothing open. So it was bad luck when I came marching into the train station at Portello, pack on and a walking stick I had found, and ran smack into a Chilean copper. And I was carrying a small amount of pot.

Jailed

It was obvious where I was coming from so the copper asked me to show him my passport. At first it seemed that it would be as Nesel said. I explained that I had walked in from Argentina and that this was the first place I had encountered in Chile where there were any officials. We went into the hotel where I changed some money and waited to get my passport stamp.

Portello was very international and jet-settish with people making arrangements to fly back to England and other distant parts.

I waited in the lobby for the cop to return. About an hour later he came back saying that it would be necessary for me to leave for Santiago. I was shocked, showed him my ticket and explained I only had a day or two to ski before I had to fly to Quito, but to no avail.

Then I started to get apprehensive. I asked them to let me find Nesel saying I had to return his clothing to him. I found him and he came upstairs and talked to the cop, who was a friend of his and found out that it was all right for me to go only as far as a police station in a mining town in the valley—Los Andes, I believe was the name. I managed to slip Nesel the film canister containing the weed, which he was most happy to receive.

So off we went at the bottom of the mountain below the snow, this cop and I were let off to wait for a bus. We were getting along pretty well talking about the "lolas" the "chicks" as I told him in English.

It was cold and the bus wasn't coming so I stuck out my thumb and much to his amusement we were picked up by this cat in a Land Rover.

At the police station things got tense for a few minutes. I did my best to explain. They were joking around with me. One cop held a Thomson submachine gun on me while another drew his revolver and told me to sing. I was shocked—though I had reason to be shocked, what with all the horror stories I had heard about Chile.

Torture, people disappearing and never heard from again.

These cats were like good ol' boys, just like prep school. They fed me and this one cop started giving head to an asparagus spear so I played along and asked him about his kids which got all the boys laughing.

One big fat copper, the one who held the revolver on me and said "canto", was named Charles. He kept trying to act super tough around me but I just shined him on and acted super friendly.

I was a bit freaked out though, like they had these posters on the wall "*¡Cuidado con los estranjeros!*" and a picture of a group of longhairs that could have been me and my friends at any time in the last five years. Fortunately, I had just gotten my hair cut and had a plane ticket (from Santiago to Quito) so I guess they thought I was legit or C.I.A. and not to be interfered with. Though they could have done anything they wanted with me; for all anyone knew I was in Argentina still.

Bang—bye. Jeff disappears without a trace.

Chile is an extremely paranoid and jumpy place and with good reason. As Hegel ascertained the history of society is change. The old is challenged by the new and is combined with the result being a mixture of the two. Thesis–Antithesis–Synthesis. Thus the history of any society is one of gradual revolution. While this is a vital process the result can be detrimental in the short run if the revolution manifests itself in the form of civil war or coup d'etat. For while the nation may be following a natural course, the sudden burst of change, flood of passion cannot help but sweep the innocent people in great numbers to death or ruin. But the absolute headspin for a people is revolution-counter revolution one-two punch.

Chile is an example. Whereas the Indochina conflicts are more violent and distinctive, the outcome is not yet known and if the insurrection should succeed in Cambodia it is doubtful that a right wing counter-revolution will be able to be maintained with the same ferocity as has been the Communist drive for power. The countries of Indochina, I believe, are after 20 years of continual war just too wasted to maintain a popular movement to the right.

Chile, however, has the unique distinction from what I know of being the only country in recent history to have gone within four years –right–left–right. The result of this in practical terms is that the left under Allende moved in, ripped off a number of people to institute their changes (some argue not enough), but Allende represented the only democratically elected Marxist in history and the leader of a popular party in a country with a previously strong democratic history.

He is faulted by other Marxists for not following one of the most basic tenets of that credo which is when you seize power coalesce it quickly and brutally and suppress all dissent and above all that greatest of fears of a communist—Maoist or Marxist, the counter-revolutionary.

This mistake was not made by the generals (Chilean military) who in full view of the guests of the fancy Sheraton Hotel across the street attacked with fighter planes and armor the Palace of the President, killed Allende and completed a successful counter-revolution.

Once in power the generals set about ripping off their selected group of people. So the poor people of Chile in the end with all the radical politics ended up with a near ruined economy (+300% inflation) and uncertain civil liberties. It is no wonder that a year after the counter-revolt, the place was still jumpy.

I am not certain of the extent of the involvement of the C.I.A. and I.T.T., copper interest in the counter-revolt, though it is widely rumored that the C.I.A. paid for a crippling truck strike and greatly supported anti-Allende forces.

The U.S. government's stated policy is to support stability in foreign governments, particularly underdeveloped ones, for they correctly realize that continual radical changes in government only weakens the social fabric—which is people wanting to know that what they are working for will not be swept away.

For the purpose of stability the U.S. Government seems to prefer the right-wing groups. But while I hope only for the people of beautiful Chile to be secure and prosperous, I also realize that if they are right-wing governed now that they will by the nature of history be pulled back to the left. Please though let the trend be gentle and slow. Let the U.S. Government have the wisdom to see the inevitability of change and use whatever clout it has to make such change gradual. For that I believe is what is best for the people.

After feeding me I was put in a cell and left there for the night. The cell stank of piss, but was much more modern than anything I would have ever encountered in the majority of South America. I pity the stupid *norteamericanos* who get caught smuggling dope and have to spend years and years in conditions infinitely worse than this cell. The profit one makes on buying cocaine or grass is tremendous if you can get it back to the U.S. We met a few people down there who were doing it and many people up here asked why I didn't try it. As it turned out my bag was never thoroughly searched and I probably could have gotten away with it, but I would much rather be poorer and free than even take the chance of having to spend five years (a light sentence) or even five days in a latino calaboza. I would pay more than I could ever make from drugs to escape that fate.

In the morning they let me out of my cell and told me they were moving me. I still did not know if I was to be released. Around mid-day Sunday, El Capitán drove with me about 30 kms more down the mountain to a government official's office.

I again explained my case. Again there was the poster "beware of foreigners." I wrote a letter while we waited for the official stamper to come in. I wrote my mother explaining what happened.

[This letter caused a sensation in Washington when my mother used her formidable government connections to inquire of the

Chilean government if I had been arrested.]

The lady didn't come so finally another official stamped my passport and I was free. God it felt great, what a relief—even though it was only 15 hours in custody I felt like I had escaped some horrible gripping fate.

I bought some food and hitched part of the way and caught a bus back to the police station where I had spent the night. It was getting late and I still had to get up the mountain.

Having been released from custody of the Chilean law with a stamped passport, I had by nightfall gotten back to the bottom of the mountain leading up to Portillo.

The bus let this girl who was going to work up at the resort and I off about a hundred meters before a military checkpoint. We walked up to it as it was a good place to get a ride. The girl got a ride quickly which is always the way in hitchhiking anywhere in the world.

I waited and talked with the soldiers. They were nice guys interested in dope stories and girls. We were getting along well marching around and playing with their guns. They finally got me a ride a small way in the back of a truck going up to a restaurant right at the beginning of the snow.

From there I caught a ride with a family going up a bit further to get some snow for playing. I kept seeing all these cars toting back big pieces of snow to Santiago. A souvenir I guess.

By now it was about dark and no ride in sight, so rather than get caught out in the open I hitched a ride back to the restaurant.

There I made friends with this beautiful Chilean girl who said she knew some people across the road I could probably stay with.

I went across the way and found this Brazilian cat and his Canadian wife. I ended up staying with them in this road tending station. Great hospitality. I just poured out my story and they were amazed.

We all went back to this restaurant where there were two other couples on a pre-wedding honeymoon. We all got drunk (not me so much but they sure tied it on) and I played music for them while this one super *borracho* raved about how he loved his country and how hard it had been the last few years. It was funny because he started talking about the beautiful girls of Chile and his intended was obviously getting madder and madder but he was too drunk to perceive it. I went over and started talking to my beautiful friend. She was pretty but I did not have the vocabulary or time to do anything about it though it was obvious she liked me a lot (or so I hoped).

In the morning I caught a ride on an army truck that was hauling beef up to the post next to Portillo. It was open back and I huddled under the tarpaulin with the frozen meat. By the time we got to the top of the mountain I was a piece of frozen meat myself.

I looked into staying at the hotel, which was like any big ski lodge, expensive. Just down the road was a small hostel for about one third of the price so I went there and was made very comfortable by the proprietor who as far as I could tell spent all day getting drunk with the locals while his wife did all the work. Needless to say he seemed a happy fellow.

I skied that afternoon but the runs were quite icy and I didn't feel confident enough to go up to the higher, more difficult trails. I did not have a good time. I seem to be stuck at a point at skiing where I will go for a day or two and just get back to where I am enjoying myself and feeling confident then I won't go for another year and have to start over again—no progress.

I spent the evening drinking and playing music for the locals. It was very nice indeed.

The next day I caught the bus to Santiago. On the way down we ran smack into a truck. We finally got disengaged and had to drive to the nearest police station.

You guessed it! It was the very same establishment where I had been incarcerated a few short days before. Well it was like old homecoming week. That big fat tuna, Charles, was there trying to act as tough as ever. Most everyone on the bus was a foreign tourist so they all stayed out on the bus while I chatted it up with the boys back at the station.

On the way to Santiago, I listened very condescendingly to the patter of the richies about their three week specials—their tidbits about Machu Picchu, Buenos Aires. I had become an incredible snob about being so much more enlightened and in touch than the jet setters.

As it turned out I was sitting next to this old Hungarian expatriate who now lived in Puerto Rico and worked for the U.S. Government. He presented a case for wanting to see as much as possible in as short as time. Time is money, etc. I could see his point being an old gent. That's why I want to do all my traveling young—slow and easy.

The bus kept breaking down and the richies were irritated to distraction. To me it seemed quite normal. They all fidgeted and wasted all this energy complaining. Finally to their fortune another empty mini-bus passed by while we were broken down on the side of the road and took us all to Santiago.

While my erstwhile companions piled into the Sheraton I went off and found a comfortable cheapie and went out for a fine meal that even included a trio playing and singing around the floor.

The waiter kept after me to hurry and finish my pollo on account of the curfew. They had to close the restaurant by 11 so they could get home by one. Anyone caught on the street after that would be put away. Santiago was a jumping city so the curfew was a hard blow to its abundant nightlife.

I set out in the morning to look at the city. I thought since I only had one day, I'd take an American Express tour. So I proceeded to the Sheraton and found out the tour was too expensive but got a map of the tour's route and decided to walk.

The Sheraton was on the same plaza as the Presidential Palace where Allende made his last stand while jets swept down past the Sheraton on their bomb runs. While tanks rolled outside I went up to the top of the hotel to try to get a view down at the palace.

Up top I found a very fancy solarium restaurant around a pool with perfect views of the gutted ruins of the palace. The scene was so cosmopolitan and I was up to get a peek at the remains of a social freakout that I decided to stay and eat breakfast. The meal was expensive but good and I was quite hungry.

I fantasized about the reaction of the rich American jet setters who a year before had been sitting there sipping their martinis as the jets swooped down past them unloading bombs on the palace below. What a freakout.

I asked the waiter and he described how the jets came in (a story I am sure he had told a few hundred times before) and how the guests stood for a moment in complete shock and then dived as one under the table. He told of only a few diners but in my imagination I saw a room full of fat bankers and matronly ladies with big hats scurrying around in panic. I believe I actually at some point during my breakfast had a fleeting sorrow that I had not been there myself.

I left the hotel and walked up the main street, O'Higgins or some ridiculously inappropriate Irish name. Santiago has a terrible smog problem. I could see two blocks in front of me to this mountain in the middle of the city, which is the main park.

I finally found it, but not until I had stumbled upon another small mountain that was built into a fort or monastery, the latter I presume. I also found the art museum, which was mostly old portraits of Spanish ancestors, not my favorite variety of the brush stroke.

I finally got on the correct path and was on the way when gazing up I was startled to see the Andes through a break in the smog. The mountains are large and magnificently beautiful. Their high snow-capped peaks hug the city, but with the ocean bordering the other side of the city a thermal inversion layer is created that produced the worst smog I have ever seen—worse than either L.A. or San Francisco, but then I wasn't there to see a clear day.

So I did the next best thing. I took a cab with some American high school students who were on an exchange program to the top of the big mountain in the center of the city. The peak is all landscaped and has a funicular, which wasn't running at the time. At the top is the proverbial Christ figure and a fantastic view of the mountains and the city.

One of the high school students was a young lady who in a typical high school way became infatuated with me and a half-hour after she met me was declaring her eternal love. While it was very flattering I felt obligated to discourage her from deserting her classes and going off with me. I told her I was leaving the next morning. She took my hand and pressed it to her ample young breast and as a tear rose to her eye and trickled down her rosy cheek, these words she did speak: "Baby, don't go, don't leave me this way."

So she and I parted; me gladly and she broken-hearted.

I then did what I think is the best way to get the feel of a city in short time: caught a crosstown bus and rode it back and forth through the bustling centro to the poor shanty areas that invariably surround Latin American cities.

It was from these barrios of oppression that either government felt the most obvious stings of their failure to provide for the welfare of the national economy. Most of the Latin American countries are rich enough to raise themselves and all the people to affluence but past interest and an all too readiness to protect the interest of the few who are rich and waste the capital of the country on arms and luxuries imported from the industrialized countries, leave the governments detached or incapable of dealing with the pressing needs of the populace. Since the only thing resembling prosperity is to be found in the big cities the poor flock there living in horrid squalor. Yet they stay—shining shoes, selling tacos, committing petty crimes. Any house of means is a fortress with high walls with broken glass at the top.

[I've decided to write a novel—which you will find in a few pages—so bye-bye reader. Here's a synopsis of the rest of the trip.]

I flew to Ecuador, met Jon and Jerry in Quito, and we traveled by land back to the good ol' USA.

Was recognized by a girl at the American Express office in Quito who had gone to my high school in AIS. We went to Colombia.

Almost busted (shot) by the cops in Bogotá. [Here, I will deviate from my rule not to inject my 38-year old memories into this account, for the Bogotá story has been repeated many times and I believe that I retain enough memory of the details to do the tale justice.]

It was the night that Richard Nixon resigned. We were crossing a park on the way to the U.S. Embassy to watch his resignation speech. On the way we went behind a row of bushes bordering a tennis court to smoke a joint.

I was leading Jerry and Jon out of the bushes when there standing before me was a uniformed cop, pistol aimed at my chest.

He probably smelled the weed on us, but fortunately we had already consumed what we had with us.

By this time in our journey we were dressed in various pieces of clothing we'd picked up along the way, including a very colorful Ecuadorian poncho I was wearing—easily identified as gringo travelers and easy picks for shaking down by the cops. Jerry and I

Six months after start return to
Santa Barbara in a Peruvian poncho

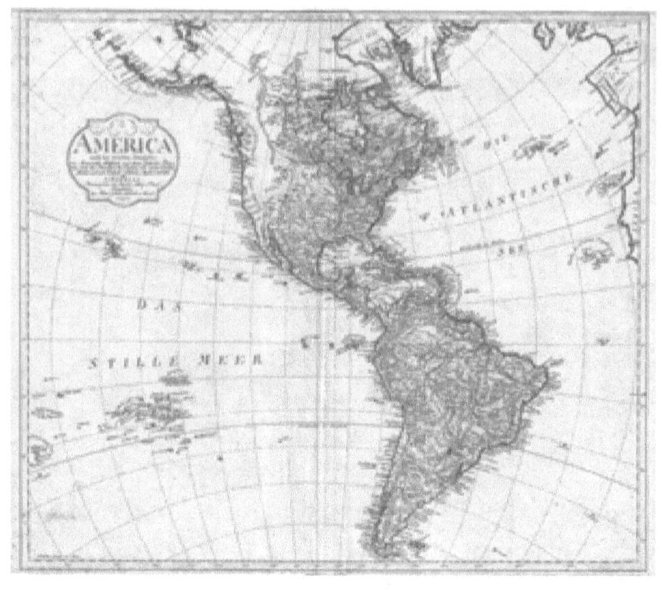

Freedom Pure Freedom

JK in dashiki

were later busted by a cop on a train in Mexico after we'd smoked a jay in a car with open windows that brilliantly for us had wafted through into other cars on the train. Like most of the cops that hassled us on the trip, it was not so much for the dope, but the chance to extract a large fine from us, or be arrested—some choice.

The Colombian cop searched us and found this canister of pepper spray I had in my pocket. I almost told him it was perfume in hopes that he might dose himself, but with him holding a gun on me, I didn't think that was such a great idea and warned him not to spray it on himself.

In the end, due to J.K.'s trusty old diplomatic passport, we were able to talk our way out it, but not before he'd ripped us off, including J.K.'s Swiss Army knife.

Where the story got funny was, being idiots, we felt as if we should report the cop who had taken J.K.'s knife, and went to the police station the next morning, presented Jon's diplomatic passport and asked to speak to the captain.

When he heard our story, he lined all the cops up in a courtyard and asked us to identify the culprit who'd robbed us.

All these porkers were obviously pissed off to be lined up in the police station courtyard and have their usual prey, gringo hippies, become the hunters. Jerry and I were loving it. We'd walk by one, turn, step closer, examine his face, walk on a few steps, spin and go back, examine them again until we couldn't maintain any longer and it all turned into a joke. Even the cops were smiling at our performance.

Needless to say we never got our stuff back, but did get out of

Colombia in one piece.

And so some quick highlights of the rest of the trip include:

- Camped in a coconut grove on the Caribbean coast of Colombia. (with a kid from West Virginia who was waiting to be taken up into the pot growing region, with hopes of making a great connection).

- Went to an island (San Andrés).

- Costa Rica—beautiful women.

- Guatemala—beautiful clothes, cheap food. Went to Tikal—amazing ruins.

- On the train ride from Mexico City to the border, we were busted again for smoking a joint, but were able to bribe our way out of it.

Six months after I left, I returned to Santa Barbara to find my father still alive. He was to live another year. I regret that I never showed him this account even though he was there as I wrote it. He was the originator of the Peace Corps concept and wrote the proposals to Congressman Henry Reuss and Senator Hubert Humphrey that resulted in the legislation founding the Peace Corps. He would have appreciated my observations and education from the ground level.

1

Bob Gete had come to Washington thirty years before as an intern during the wide-eyed New Deal days. He had helped draft the Marshall Plan and other programs including the one he had proposed and developed, the Peace Corps. Made his career as an official of the Agency for International Development. Bob had a simplistic theory that was in actuality the curious urge to experiment allowed to one recently retired from a long distinguished career.

As he walked into the cavernous lobby and passed by the large population board that continually churned out new birth and death statistics, he formulated his presentation to the Secretary.

It was Bob's idea that for the actual price of a small scale war every member of the warring country could be made rich.

"Vietnam," he told the Secretary, "was costing a billion a week at one point. Hell, it would have been cheaper for us to build a high-rise in Iowa for each and every family in both North and South Vietnam. At least it would have been good for the housing industry."

"Bob, if I didn't have the highest regard for your accomplishments," murmured the Secretary.

"I'm not suggesting we actually cover Iowa with high-rises." They both laughed at the notion of a Viet Cong guerilla ordering a pizza sent over to his high-rise.

"Yet what is it we've been pursuing in our A.I.D. programs? We have always approached the problem from one point. We provide assistance in the hopes that those assisted will develop."

"Develop what?"

"The first thing they want is a car, roads and a shopping center. It's my suggestion that we try it from the other end. In the Peace Corps we've had interesting results with our kids coming back with more tempered and objective views on where they want their own culture to go. Admittedly they often found our values to be at fault. But what is important is that elements of our middle class were encouraged toward a worldwide perspective and gotten out of Iowa. It is this intelligence and experience among the general populace, which will support democratic government in a mutually dependent world."

"Fine, Bob, you can save the eloquence for the House Committee."

Bob grinned as he too realized that he had been jabbing his finger in the air and articulating in his best speech posture.

"What's your proposal, Bob? No, let me guess, you want us to go out and build shopping malls all over the world."

Bob thought, you smug son of a bitch. "No, I want to staff out a project to be like a reverse Peace Corps. You bring a few average third-world types into the U.S. for two years so that they can go back and spread the word among the populace about what we're like. I don't know if you've noticed but every popular movement in the last 20 years has been markedly anti-American. It's the elites who always stand up for us and why? Because many of them have been here to visit or for school and found out what a crazy mixed up bundle of stuff this country is. Does wonders to relieve feelings of conspiracy and paranoia to switch the channels of a TV on a Sunday afternoon. I also think it's crucially important at this time for the, if you'll excuse the expression, 'masses of the world' to stop thinking of us as all men who walk on the moon and all women who live in penthouses with handsome suitors calling. Have you ever gone to the movies in Latin America? A very popular form of entertainment—all American B movies. My God, the popular opinion of an American is someone who can't go walking down the street without getting in a fight, falling in love or seeing a Martian."

He was gesturing forcefully, punctuating his arguments with smiles and looks of encouragement to make sure that Secretary Stanley was listening. He radiated harmony, body and mind humming at the same frequency. And the Secretary found it impossible not to be interested in his argument, if not for what he was saying, but for his style. Stanley had learned a long time ago on the Choate Debate Team to respect those forensic points most that sparkled and snapped like electricity as they flowed out. If Gete had walked in and ruminated a staff memo spitting out salivary cud at him, he would have turned off long ago. As it was he found himself arguing along that U.S.I.A. had spent billions to explain American ways of life but to a great extent had not reached the majority of the people in the country.

The Secretary had, through a judicious contribution, gotten himself an ambassadorship. He had met Gete while serving what became a distinguished and productive tour in Zaire. The fact that he had performed so ably had effectively removed him from the ranks of the relatively ignoble political appointee to one respected by the pros and eventually his Cabinet post. He respected Bob and had a vague inkling that Bob was much his intellectual superior but his ego, conditioned by private schools and tempered by honest achievement, soon had him talking of the idea with minor adjustments, as if it were his own.

As Bob left the office on his way to lunch with a senior Senator he had once coached on the intricacies of foreign affairs, he remembered an old mentor's admonishment that a new program was not a baby. It was crucial that a proposal have as many fathers as was credible. Let Humphrey claim he originated the idea for the Peace Corps and let the others claim that it was theirs. Gete got his satisfaction from the results. He was well known and respected enough to gain entrance into all the right doors. Indeed it was more often the famous and powerful who sought him out for advice. Gete treasured and protected his anonymity. He found the TV lights and the recognition on the street a decided handicap. Gete was more than happy to settle for the greater privacy. The lack of competition for the limelight with those who craved the recognition, their name on a law, allowed Getz, as his mentor Averell Harriman had put it, to plant the seed of a program with the touch of a ghost and the spark of a muse.

Emerging from the cab in front of the old Senate office building he thought of his most cherished successes and then of the same debacle. They balance each other out he thought. It was this balance he had sought throughout his life; the golden mean. It was the same equilibrium he tried to help bring to the world—not the ideal communism—how boring if everyone had the same thing. No, let there be poor and rich, fast and slow. But not in such great disproportion as existed today. Yes a world of . . .

"Senator Steeple would like to see you now, Mr. Gete."

* * *

"Frank, what we want to get is the real thing." Gete addressed the senator. "As you know the Peace Corps was quite successful in its original endeavor to get around the elite-to-elite association that still persists."

"You mean," the senator joined in, "Ivy League graduates getting together at embassies and thinking they represent their various countries?"

"Exactly," Gete urged him on. He was never sure if the senator was more the apt student or rather a master of the political art of seeming to agree with your core beliefs. Gete decided he was innately a learner—a paramount quality in those who would lead—and that his political skills were growing.

"So we take non-elites from down there and bring them up here for an exposure to developed life." Gete cringed at the world "developed." He had seen one government official after another blow any chance for rapport with a third world representative by the use of the word underdeveloped. Of course most of the time the so-called third world representative was trained in an American college and was quite sold on the idea that his homeland was third rate. Rather than develop beautiful spots in his own country they invariably, it seemed to Gete, wasted their money in the

Fontainebleau in Miami Beach, or in the casinos in Monte Carlo.

"I think it's a fine idea Bob and I'll try and write in some funds for it into the next foreign aid package."

That's fine for now, Bob thought, but it was better for later. Gete had a pretty good idea that he was talking to the next President of the United States and he was not surprised when two years later the Person-to-Person Corps was one of the best-liked aspects of the platform which Steeple successfully ran on for his bid for the Presidency.

2

On a narrow strip of sand crowded between the Pacific Ocean on the west and the towering Andes Codillera on the east lay a small stretch of desolation. The weather in this spot is particularly droll and uncompromising due in full to a perpetual disagreement between ocean and air currents. The Humboldt Current, swinging northward from Antarctica brushes the coast with a broad layer of cold water. The anchoveta find this a delightful environment and flock there quite as regularly as do New Yorkers to Florida. The prevailing southerly winds are cooled as they cross the offshore current. Upon reaching shore the air warms, increasing its capacity for moisture and evaporates the water of the coastal strip rather than depositing moisture on it. The air must be cooled in the altitude of the Andes before the moisture gathered on the coast is released. The resulting atmosphere on the coast is humid and often overcast but no rain falls. In the winter months of July and August humidity may reach the point where the air turns misty and paved surfaces glisten with dampness but this alone is not enough to support more than an occasional epiphyte, which is an airborne plant.

The coast is a desert. Transecting the coast are some 52 rivers and streams. Because of the lack of rainfall all agriculture is carried on by means of irrigation. This has been so since very early times.

Dick Keating drove the A.I.D. mission car south from Trujillo, through Moche, climbed out of the valley and into the coastal desert. He was on his way to pick up one Birú Pizango and transport him to Lima.

Once in Lima, Birú would be given a six-week training program and then transported to the United States as one of the first Reverse Peace Corps initiates. Keating had made the trip before. The two-lane strip stretched before him like a heavy black shoelace curling and contouring around the sand dunes and boulder-filled gullies. In spots the desert moving northeasterly encroached on the black strip and covered it with greyish-gold shifting sand. An occasional clump of dark spiny grass would struggle to hold the sand and gravel. Three enormous sand dunes marched like giant mastodons from the sea. As he drove past the stark black peaks erupting suddenly from the sand, he found the lunar panorama to be a beautiful sight to drive by, but to live there? How could anyone?

Suddenly over a rise the Viru valley lay before him. Its green form was sharply drawn by a far irrigation ditch, on one side sand and the other verdant plants. Fragile peasant huts of wattle and daub marked the homes of the *campesinos*. It was from one of these barrios that Birú was coming.

When the program was first announced all the local gentry had immediately assumed that it would be one of the sons or daughters who would journey to the United States. The daughter of the director of the Banco de Nación, Magalay Mojica, had gone to high school in the U.S.A. for a year and was now at the Catholic University in Lima. Indeed there was much talk in the town and by the hacienda owners who would get this great adventure which so obviously would lead to better things in life.

Señor Vaati, owner of the hacienda el Trujillo, had good reason to believe that his son Manuel would be chosen. After all, he did have a brother in the Foreign Office and a cousin in San Francisco though he had never met the fellow. It was Manuel who first told him about the program. He had heard it from the Peace Corps *gringo* who came to give medicine to the *campesinos*. "That would stop soon, heh," he thought. Not medicine but birth control he gave them. No more Madre Dios. He was not sure about this birth control thing—the Church was against it so it was bad. But the mamas were now not always pregnant and took better care of the other kids—so more lived. Don Vaati was sure that there were fewer babies now which meant fewer *campesinos* to work his land in later years. He promised himself to talk to the priest tomorrow.

Manuel came walking up and told him some unbelievable news. The *gringo* had come and talked to the family of Birú Pizango and now Pizango was *borracho* on chicha saying his son was going to the United States and soon the whole family would be rich.

"*Hijo de puta!*" Vaati exclaimed upon hearing the news. "You think he's just drunk?" he asked his son.

"He says a man is coming today, a *gringo* to go with Birú and guide him," Manuel replied. "Birú's working in the field like always."

"Get me this peasant! He's got no money to leave here. He must stay and work. *Chica de madre,*" he muttered and he walked back to the house. He was a swarthy man, broad of back. He imagined himself a king, which in a sense he was. The hacienda was almost self-sufficient and those who lived and worked on the land did so by the grace of his word. But he had seen things change in his lifetime—pressure without and within. Once his father had owned the whole valley and his great grandfather's father had been the heir to the north half of Peru.

His ancestor conquistador Vaati had been a member of a ragtag bunch of cutthroats who had been in the right place at the right time when two Inca brother kings got to feuding. The Quito bro told the Spaniards how to find Cuzco—so they lay waste to Cuzco then came back and mopped up on Quito. Historians have often wondered how it was that such a rabble of wayfarers could desolate a mighty kingdom that had stood for centuries. A few years back they found some mummies and discovered it was the clap, and the common cold, plus the plain surprise of seeing men riding around all done up in armor on horses and toting things on carts. You see the Inca never did invent the wheel being they were mostly mountain folk. Yet they were able to move giant masses of precisely cut rock for miles over mountains, then fit them together to form mighty structures. It's a secret that's been kept to this day. The heir to this great conquest stepped on to the porch to confront the heir of those conquered.

The youth stood silently before him. Though fully grown he was slight of stature, bronze-skinned with dark straight hair.

"Heh *calabaza,* idiot, answer me."

The youth gazed back at him with the same friendly blank stare that was so prevalent among his people.

"This is nonsense" thought Vaati, and decided to change his

tact. "Well young man I have known you since you were a *niño, sí*? And your family, your family has worked these lands for my family since the times before our grandfathers, *sí*?? I am your patrón. Tell me what have you been talking to the *gringa* about?"

"*Sí, señor,*" the youth replied just a hint of focus coming into his eyes.

"How did you come to know her?"

"*La escuela,*" the youth haltingly replied.

Asul, that damn school, he had tried to stop it from being built. The *gringos* had come with money and built a school and now the government sent teachers. Teaching *calabazas* to read was like teaching pigs to fly, he had admitted once while drunk and had liked the phase so much that he had used it many times, always condemning the school to Hades when he was through. Indeed, the very mention of the school set him off on a soliloquy that ended five minutes later with the lowly Quonset hut again being dispatched to the fires of hell.

The youth, who was already intimidated, was now speechless and wandered back to the field. He loved the school and rose early in the morning to have enough time to study his books. As it was, he only now had a few hours a week to spend learning there. But lately the *gringa*, Nancy, had spent time teaching him English. Many times at the *cine* he had seen movies of the United States and thought now of going there. The idea did not seem real. The hombres and guns, and other screen images of cars and busy streets filled his head. He was scared of going and now the thought of leaving his family left him convinced that he would not soon be leaving his home.

He felt comforted by his own reassurances and laughed to himself at how he would tell his *campaneros* the story of Don Vaati talking of the school. His eyes got this big, he laughed and puffed his cheeks out and shook his jowls in a fair but definitely unflattering imitation of the don Vaati. That man is *loco*, no?

His heart got lighter and his eyes drank in the familiar surroundings of the hacienda. It was as if he were seeing them in a new way. Like when he thought he had lost his favorite satchel of woven fibers and then found it again. Now he took so much better care of it. But his new happiness was short-lived as he rounded the corn patch by his family's hut and saw a big *gringo* car parked in the dirt road a half-mile from the house. He sensed what it meant and turned in sudden panic to run. But as he ran down the path through the fields he ran right into his father leading a burro loaded with cut wood, a valuable cargo in the desert.

"*Venga*, Birú, *mira* the *gringo* is here. *Mi hijo*, my son, I am so proud of you. You, my little Birú, will go and learn how to be rich!"

"Papa" Birú stuttered, "I don't want to go." He started to cry.

"*Madre Dios*," the father sighed holding his trembling son in his arms. "Birú, Birú, *mi hijo*, we live like the pigs, we have nothing. You can change this. Only you. Nothing will get better. Your *madre*, she is so proud. I, I am not glad to see you go, but Birú my son, you must. You must."

He took his son by the shoulder and walked him back up to the hut. There, in front of the wood and tin hovel his mother was bent over the open fire, cooking *chifles* to sell in the market. Her youngest baby was wrapped to her back with an old woven cloth,

His brothers and sisters played in the dirt. A skinny dog yelped away as a younger brother threw a rock at him. Chickens flurried as the dog ran through them. And there to the side wall the *gringa* Nancy and another *gringo* he had never seen before.

Jolly up a tree

3

Dick Keating took a toke off a joint of Colombian and drove down past the grand black dunes and into the Viru valley stretching like a twenty-mile golf course. He laughed to himself, only here grass traps were surrounded by links of sand. The valley ran from a narrow end against the mountains to broad beaches at the sea. As Keating drove along the beach the breakers seemed to be coming in from an odd direction. His old surfing instincts reemerged and he properly noted that the breaks were all right with the swell from the south. He felt the old instinct to pull off the road and jump into his wetsuit, grab his board and paddle out into the eight foot swell just as he used to while driving home to Santa Barbara from up north. His mind flashed back to trips to Hollister Ranch and pulling over the pass to find a good break at Gaviota or El Cap.

As he pulled into view of the town of Viru he passed a nice beach break with good even sets rolling in. Couldn't surf here, he calculated. I'd have to go down-current from that town and all their shit. I'd be dodging turds out there, he laughed.

The town streets were cobblestones with a few one or two story plaster edifices bordering a permanent market used by small property owners who cultivated plots of the surrounding land. Many of them lived in the town in two residential barrios. In the center of the town was the proverbial church, plaza, and headquarters of the dominant political party.

Keating parked the car and walked into a small grocery and restaurant arrangement. The floor was dirt and the roof was so low he had to bend his lanky frame to keep from scraping his head as he had done a few times before to the great amusement of the Lilliputian natives. In a corner was a stove tended by a fat Indian woman dressed in the beautiful woven garment that seemed to be so common, yet each was distinct and had probably been with the owner for some time, judging from the wear on it. Another younger version of the Indian cook came over and took his order for eggs and rice plus a *gaseoso*. She returned soon with the food and a pink drink called Inca cola.

"Not this shit," he thought. "*No tienes* coca cola?"

"*No señor.*"

"Man this stuff is weird!" he exclaimed half out loud. "Tastes like liquid bazooka gum." He had drunk it once before and once was enough.

"Traígame me una cerveza, por favor."

"*¿Qué?*" she said, giving him that blank uncomprehending stare reserved for *gringos* and other *estranjeros* who do things incomprehensible like order a soft drink then ask to be brought a beer.

"Yo no care esto gaseoso, no me gusta Inca cola."

Again the questioning look but this time she humbly took the cola back.

He noticed that it had been partially opened for him. He felt bad and considered telling her to just go ahead and leave it but decided that would confuse her even further. I'll leave a big tip to cover the price of the cola, he thought.

As he sat waiting for his food to arrive he saw a *gringa* girl walk by on the street. Though he had come to the point of seeing Indian beauty in its own light, the sight of an American or European female always brought his thoughts into the present and focused them, at least momentarily, in that peculiar mixture of desire and critique that lately blew across the consciousness he had yet to develop for Indian women. Particularly at this moment he was startled by the realization first that the woman was a *gringa*, second that she was black, and third that he knew her. "Nancy," he called as he ran out the door.

"Dick, I didn't expect you until tomorrow."

"Yeah, I got done in Tumbes early and split—hate that place."

"Yeah, I don't blame you." She tried to act glad to see him—but the truth was, if he could have perceived it, that she resented him professionally on account of the continued rivalry between the Peace Corps and the A.I.D. Program. "We bust our asses in the field while the A.I.D. people sit in offices and worry about their careers." Personally, she had found Keating to be a bit of a drag. She had seen him in Lima at the embassy sporting the standard embassy coat and tie and uptight decorum. Now, however, he seemed transformed simply by the fact that he was dressed in jeans and hiking boots. Though she liked his field demeanor better than the embassy professional she still thought him attitude toward the project was a bit condescending and "We're the pros from America who are going to fix your problems." There is a difference when you work directly with people. You don't see them so much as "projects." He no longer threatened or disgusted her as did the "elder statesmen" usually associated with A.I.D. and the State Department. He had become to her a misguided friend, someone to be convinced of the error of his ways.

As they drove out of town in the Peace Corps jeep, she tried to give him a quick synopsis of her experiences accumulated during her year and a half working in and around the valley. Because she was trying to convince him, her comments were editorial. Keating found her elaborations refreshing after having dealt so much with the factual precision of the incessant reports that crossed his desk in Lima. He was excited to be in the field and to be away from the diffident countenance which he assumed in his work. He played an effective game at his work but it was a role he had not yet grown accustomed to. Being out in the *campo* with this girl restimulated a side of his personality with which he was familiar and confident.

"Most of the people in this area are little more than serfs."

"Are you a revolutionary?" he asked a bit sardonically. He acted as an antagonist for the sake of the argument, though basically he agreed with her.

"You are damn right," she said.

"Look at Chile," he argued, "they suffered more from the revolution than they'll gain back in five years."

"That was no revolution" she retorted. "The only true revolution in Latin America was Cuba. These coups and countercoups are jive, just more power-brokering between various military and economic factions. Jive, shit," she spat out.

"You seem quite bitter" he assuaged, placing some concern in his inflection.

"I've lived with these people, man. I've seen the traps that hold them down and nothing is going to change until these people organize, rise up and seize their land and their rights."

"Why do you associate yourself with an offshoot of the U.S. government?" he asked, genuinely curious as to what brought the woman to this valley.

"You mean what's a black woman doing in Peru?" she asked.

"You must get asked that a lot, but I am curious," he said.

They were now stopped at a checkpoint at Puente de Viru. She gazed off absently at fat Indian women who sat under cloth awnings shielding them from the harsh glare of the sun, and sold fruit and other foods to passing motorists.

"I was raised in D.C., got a scholarship to American University and majored in Latin American studies. It just always seemed right to me. Third world solidarity," she muttered, as if pained at how euphemistic the phrase sounded. How absurd when gazing at the grinning, chattering Indian women and trying to imagine them marching arm in arm with Nancy down the boulevard of radical social change at the vanguard of the revolution. "I realize now that if I help these people to start using their minds, they will break out of the malnourishment traps that keep them stupid."

"What do you mean, stupid?" he asked.

"I mean," she explained, "that many of these people suffer

irreversible mental retardation at an early age from malnourishment and then raise their kids poorly and are unable to produce enough to get by, so they live everyday like you feel when you've got a bad case of the flu."

"I get you," he said, "down and lethargic."

"If these people ever get to a point where they can start thinking up to their potential, there won't be anything that can hold them back when they figure out what's going on."

"What about those Indians there?" he asked, pointing to the group that were selling to the crowds. "They seem to be engaged in good old private enterprise."

"It's a double standard. Most of their contemporaries aren't even part of the economy."

They were now driving down the Pan American Highway again. Nancy argued that the government was negligible in educating the people and was more interested in reserving their elite status than properly developing the economy.

At a sleepy old restaurant named Baldman they turned westward off the highway.

"Your notion is not one of which I am totally unaware," he said unconsciously, slipping back into his Embassy reserve. "The economy must be developed as best as possible," he said politically. Things were tense now, he wanted to tell her that he basically agreed with her feelings and admired her for acting upon them in a constructive manner. Perhaps she sensed this because the tense timbre that had been filling her voice gave way to a subtler humor that seemed to laugh at the way their roles lied so conveniently for both of them.

A silence followed that served to slightly diffuse the energies that had been winding up so tightly between them. They had turned down a dirt road full of potholes and in typically horrible disrepair.

Nancy expertly drove the car around the chuckholes and loose rock at a slow jogging pace, slow enough to avoid immediately destroying the car, but fast enough to escape the heavy clouds of dust billowing up behind. It was 4 kilometers from the turnoff to the gates of the hacienda and it took about 30 minutes for the drive. On either side of the road the field of another hacienda stretched away.

They stopped to pick up a hitchhiker. He was dressed in a poncho, short pants, and sandals and carried a bundle on his back. He seemed hesitant about getting in the car at first, but then climbed in and was all smiles and gratitude.

They let him off at a small path on the side of the road. Nancy had been chatting quite freely with him in a combination of slang Spanish and an Indian dialect which Keating did not fully understand. At a dirt byroad leading off from the road they let him off. He respectfully asked how much the ride cost, obviously expecting Nancy's rhetorical protest. *"Por nada, hombre! Hasta otro día."*

Keating began to feel that he was truly out of touch with these people as compared to Nancy and he wondered if he would have trouble communicating with Birú.

Keating then asked the question he had been itching to but had felt compelled to repress—his attitude toward race and women—to try to act as if it made no difference, but of course it did. Yet he never knew how women would react. "How does being a woman affect your dealings with these people?" he asked as nonchalantly as possible. He opted for the lesser of the two evils. She seemed to enjoy the question and paused a moment before answering.

"I was told by my trainer that I was the first black woman going to Peru. That always turns a black on, being first, you know," she said facetiously.

He responded with a quick, short laugh that was more a nervous sigh.

"When I arrived down here I was greeted with mostly curiosity and even disbelief. Primarily on account of being a Peace Corps worker, second for being female and third for being black. The latter works to my advantage now. It makes me easily recognizable."

She was throwing the lines out now as if in a speech. He was not really sure if she was trying to be funny. "They call me *La Negra*. I get by as well as anyone else," she demurred.

And indeed as they turned at the gates to the hacienda el Troijo, they were greeted after persistent honking by a gatekeeper who greeted Nancy effusively, "'*Hola Negra*." And Keating, "*Buenos días, señor*."

They drove another two kilometers along a road lined with dusty pines, a bit like southern France, Keating flashed. The *campamento* could be seen in the distance, marked by a large grove of trees all bent northward due to the always-prevailing southern breeze. The fields stretched away on both sides, planted in potatoes and corn. The whole operation looked fairly efficient to Keating. He noticed a tractor in the field and a modern diesel-powered irrigation system surrounded by straw-hatted men who looked up curiously when they drove by and waved excitedly upon recognizing Nancy. They all seemed to be laughing a chorus of *hola Negra*!

They drove by a sandy soccer field and some administrative huts. By a field of corn they parked the car and climbed a hill to a dilapidated hut where they were greeted by a dog, who slunk away suspiciously at their approach.

"Birú's parents are sharecroppers" Nancy explained as they climbed the hill. "Birú's father is named César," she continued. "He is a hard working man. Birú is the oldest of eleven children."

"My god," Keating exclaimed, "I hope you've got her on birth control."

"We try not to mention that," Nancy laughed slyly. "It was too late for the old mamacita but the kids at the school are being told that it is possible to have birth control. We don't lecture about it but it's really a popular topic of discussion."

"I'm sorry I interrupted," Keating said. "Tell me more about Birú's family."

"César has some prestige around here because he's a hot tractor driver. He sharecrops about 16 hectares of land."

They talked to the mother and Nancy hugged a number of the kids. Birú was expected back later. As Keating stood off waiting he surveyed the scene of the little adobe hut with the tin roof, the total lack of sanitation, and gazed down at the men working the fields stretching twenty miles to the sea. He was struck with the realization of what he was a part of. "We are taking someone from this and zapping them into Washington, D.C."

A car windshield flashed a reflection of the sun on the distant Pan-American Coast Highway. "This is nuts," Keating thought.

JO after three months in the Andes

4

Manuel Vaati came into his father's office to tell him the news that the *gringos* were at Birú Pizango's house this second. He was a slight, dark-haired boy of seventeen and next year he would go to Lima to the Catholic University. He was scared enough of that and did not warm to his father's verve to go to the United States. Yet he did understand that it was a matter of honor and that somehow it was a disgrace to have a mere *campesino* go from the hacienda and not him. Manuel found his father in the study engaged in a heated discussion with a man he recognized as a union leader. He could tell his father was seething yet he seemed to be treating the man with unusual diffidence. As Manuel approached he heard the union man protesting that the assigned number of rows of corn to be harvested per man was too large in view of the growth of the fields.

"Weeds!" Vaasi sputtered and started to curse under his breath.

"Let me remind you," the union man continued, "that if you fail to meet the needs of the workers you shall be subject to Land Reform. We shall nationalize these lands and form a *colectivo*. As it is," he said, "this is the wish of Lima."

Manuel started to withdraw, not wanting to be around when his father began to beat on this fellow's head as Manuel surely expected to happen. To his surprise his father, though red in the face, remained calm and called him over and said, "*señor* Castillo, may I present my son Manuel?"

Manual blushed at the unusual and strange behavior on his father's part. His father introduced the fat little man seated in front of him as the Secretary-General of the Workers Union.

Manuel nodded as he shook his hand and quite flustered, blurted out to his father that the *gringos* were at the place of Birú Pizango.

What a day for surprises. Instead of exploding, his father turned to the fat man and said. "You see *señor* Castillo, here is the boy of one of my workers who was educated at a school right here on the hacienda. Soon he will go to the United States. We are very proud of him."

Manuel could not believe it. His father almost seemed to be truly proud.

Señor Castillo, who was trying to play both ends against the middle, had been looking for an excuse to be driven around the grounds with the owner. It would not hurt, he thought, to have the workers see me being escorted by *señor* Vaasi. He therefore jumped up and said, "Come, I would like to see this family and fine young man."

"Perhaps another time," Vaasi said, obviously pained.

"No, I do not want to come north that often, I would very much like to go."

Señor Vaasi laughed nervously and swallowed some words as he sent for the horses. "Would you like a change of clothes?" he asked, noting Castillo's suit.

"No, I will drive in my car."

"Fat Pig, *Puta Gordo,* can't ride a horse," Vaasi thought to himself. But he said forcing a smile, "No, no, *señor*, we will take the hacienda car."

As they rode down the dirt road, Vaasi ignored the workers who tipped their hats as they drove by and turned to the union man who was busy waving back and as if to distract him said, "Ah, these men, hard workers! Take this fellow Pizango, hard worker, good family, ten kids, great tractor driver."

As if to add emphasis and something resembling credibility to what he was about to say next, Vaasi cleared his throat, raised his hand, and after a momentary silence declared he had tried to give Pizango the 16 hectares of land he sharecropped. "Look here,' I said, 'Take your land. It is yours now. Give me one sol, only one, yes only one sol.' But do you know what would happen if I did that? I would be a scoundrel."

"Perhaps you would prefer the Land Reform to take care of this unpleasant detail for you," Castillo laughed.

"No, no," Vaasi blustered, "they don't like it. There is not enough land to go around. The others would say, 'Why didn't you give us some land? You are not being fair to us.' And soon they would think I was a scoundrel, a *gamonal*, look at that nasty *hacendado* oppressing us. And my neighbor, *¡Madre Dios, loco!* 'You are ruining us,' they would say. 'Why are you giving your land away? Why are you being so cruel?' So, *señor* Castillo," he implored, with both hands, "it is cruel to give my land away and I cannot." But Vaasi seemed to be saying you cannot. You and your shitty land reform cannot be so cruel as to give my land to the workers. That would be cruel, not cruel to me you understand, but cruel to them.

When the two gentlemen reached the hut of Pizango, the two *gringos* were already there. The small children and animals could not believe the size of such a crowd of strangers standing at their door at one time. They peered out from back corners of the house, not having anywhere else to hide in the barren clearing the house stood on.

5

Birú Pizango looked on in helpless awe as his father humbly greeted the *americanos*. As always he was amazed at the size of a *gringo*. *Madre*, he thought, thousands of these men, maybe more. As many people as kernels of corn in the field or sand on the dunes. He shivered inside.

He liked the *gringa*, Nancy, and felt her to be a friend. He had told her once he'd like to go to the U.S. He therefore stood next to her. At one point he felt the urge to pull her aside and confess his fear. But neighbors were beginning to gather and he began to feel like a hero. He could see awe in their faces and feel respect that he had never known.

He was enjoying these new sensations with some *amigos* when a group of girls approached giggling. Many his own age were already married but he had never been able to decide on one. Among the girls laughing was one sobbing, Marisa. She was more slender than the rest with long black hair and eyes that twinkled when she laughed and she often laughed. Once she had told him she liked his moustache. Marisa was sixteen and he had felt lately that it was she that he would marry. Maybe after the next planting. Now she looked sad and he felt embarrassed because he knew that of all the people only she was sad.

Emotions and sensations were passing through Birú at a sickening rate. He felt his fear edging toward a dizzying loss of control. A large jolt of surprise turned to panic when he saw the *hacendado* park on the road and start to climb up the path accompanied by a fat stranger in a suit. Suddenly a profound relief poured over him. Vaasi had said he would never let him go! Never had he felt so glad to see the *hacendado*. In an instant his feelings of being oppressed by Vaasi turned to a feeling of security. Here was his protector, his provider.

Though they worked for him, the tenant farmers rarely had spoken to Vaasi. He was greeted with respect by the elder men with their hats in their hands.

Vaasi ignored them and went up to the *gringos*. Now, he will tell them, Birú thought. But what had been a kaleidoscope of emotions went right over the rainbow into shock, amazement, and complete terror when Birú observed the *hacendado* congenially greet the *gringos* then turn his way with the other man.

"*Señor* Castillo," Vaasi said, "here is the fine young man we are so proud of who will soon journey to the *Estados Unido*."

Birú stood thin, shocked, dumb, feeling as if every grain of sand, every bird, animal and cloud were conspiring to tear him from his home.

The other one, the mestizo government man, shook his hand and said how proud he was to see a young man like him make such a journey. Birú could barely hear him as he told of how he too had come from a farm long ago.

The two gentlemen soon left and the rest began a party, playing flutes and guitars and drinking the corn beer *chicha*. As the night fell Birú stood helpless as his friends congratulated him. Soon the men were drunk, the children playing, and the women laughing and eating corn together. The young man stood in shock and solitude off in the dark by himself. He heard footsteps behind him and turned to see Marisa standing staring at him. They looked at each other a moment. She seemed to be quivering on the spot. For a moment he felt irresistibly drawn to her but as he started to move, she sobbed and ran in terror.

"She loves me," he thought. The idea and feeling filled him—nothing else seemed to matter. In a moment he felt large and proud. He would go and become rich and come back to her.

Birú went searching for Marisa and found her weeping off near the path.

"Come," he said, taking her hand, "we will be married tonight."

She looked up at him and took his hand. They walked down the path to the cornfield and made a bed from fallen corn stalks. As they lay together she trembled as he touched her in a way no man had ever before. It was so blissful to her. But her moans of passion were caught and intermingled with sobs.

After, their bodies lying with each other, he told her that he would return to her and they would be rich.

Marisa was quiet for a moment and sobbed.

"Why would you leave?" she asked.

"I don't know" he said, "the world wants me and I do not have the power to say no."

"We can go to the witch and ask for power" Marisa said. "She is good. I asked her for you and now we are here."

"Will she have the power?" he asked with hope in his voice. "No, there is not time. I will leave in the morning."

"I will wait," she said over and over as he fell into a fitful sleep in her arms.

6

Birú woke at about 4:30 a.m. He was still overwhelmed with emotion primarily at the sight of his beautiful wife lying beside him. He lay there shivering in the cold morning and pulled his poncho close around them.

Birú got up and kissed Marisa. He walked back up to his family's house. The sight of the house and the early morning fires set waves of sorrow pouring over him. In order to lessen the impact of this, the most momentous day in his life, he set about performing his duties just as he would on any other Thursday.

Dressed in his patched and tattered work clothes, he left the house carrying a six-liter milk can. He walked quietly still in shock through the darkness nearly half a mile to a hacienda field where the family cow was pastured. Birú located the bony animal and opened the can. He filled nearly the full six liters before the udders were empty. He then pulled up the cow's stake and led her to a fresh spot in the field to graze. After re-staking the cow, Birú returned to the can of milk and carried it across the field to a spot beside the road. He knew that soon the daily truck to Trujillo would pass and pick the milk up as it did six days a week and deliver it to the milk wholesaler in town. The family received 68 centavos for this milk which was a large part of their income.

Birú returned home and washed, shaved, and ate a small breakfast of two little bread rolls and instant coffee. As he sat listening to the radio the hacienda work-bell tolled. He heard his brother pick up his shovel outside and leave for the shape-up where he would be assigned to a work detail.

Birú put on his good clothes and sat waiting with his bundle packed.

At 9:00, the *gringo* came and stood at the door. Birú rose and smiled at him meekly. They got in a car and drove out of the hacienda to the main highway and turned south to Lima. Birú looked back one time and then turned back to the road. The scenery whizzed by at a pace Birú had never known before.

A car shot past a lumbering *colectivo* full of workers. A few glared at Birú inquiringly and he smiled back.

The speed of the car and the distance that every second separated him from his home and those like him in the truck filled his veins with excitement. The dull lethargy he had felt while waiting to leave was swept behind by the emotion. He was on his way. The next hill could not be climbed fast enough for him to see what was on the other side. And though it was only desert, he saw larger hills, cities and plains. To him every second seemed like he was born again.

By evening there were cars and trucks and giant roads and then in the dark he could see lights stretching in points to the sky. Tremendous lights. Lima.

As they drove into the city, Birú was terrified and electrified at the same time.

Even if the bed at the center had not been too soft he would not have been able to sleep. The power and constant throbbing of the city swept him along at its own pace.

Birú asked the *gringo* if he could go look at the sights.

"But Birú," he said, "it is night. Wait and we will go in the morning."

So Birú had to satisfy himself with sitting in front of the building. He sat there feeling stupid, wondering at the people who looked like him yet were dressed in *norteamericano* clothes jumping in and out of cars. He closed his eyes and in the throbbing din of the city saw Marisa dressed in sparkling lights and he in pants and coat driving in a car as lights and sounds swept past them in a blur. They cling to each other in excitement and ecstasy. Then the car stops in front of the hacienda and *señor* Vaasi comes out to greet them. He welcomes them and leads them to the dining room for wine and beef.

The dreams and the miracle reality continued throughout the night. Birú dozed off and was awoken by a policeman.

"Hey, *campesino*, go sleep in the park. This place is for the *caballeros*," he said to Birú.

Birú explained to him the situation. At first he did not believe it but a *gringo* coming out the door vouched for him and the cop went away, obviously amazed and impressed. Again the new sensation of power struck Birú. He was being lifted up. Soon he would have the privilege of any *caballero*. Soon he would ride in cars, eat in restaurants and live in fine houses with soft beds.

The days passed quickly. Birú got so he could walk alone though the streets and find his way home. Once he was lost for every golden goose they've ever managed to steal." He laughed, obviously pleased with his turn of phrase.

Jim had been through Panama before. There were parts untouched by the green hand of America that were quite lovely and the people genial. But Panama City, like San Juan, Puerto Rico was a motley contrast between American commercialism and Latin culture.

The plane set down at Tocumen for a half-hour. The airport terminal was full of slot machines, a camera shop, and other tourist stores. Rather than stay inside with all that, Jim stood in the early morning sun as it sparkled off the mist rising from the jungle. Already it was quite warm and the water from a rain during the night was beginning to steam on the runway. The big American jet on the same route taxied off to the runway.

Fifteen minutes later they were airborne again flying to Cali in Colombia.

In the terminal two beautiful young ladies approached Jim and giggling shyly tried to talk to him in English. One of the thrills of traveling in Latin America was the way women looked at him. He figured his tall blond looks were attractive to Latin women because of the domination of United States movie, television, and advertising. It always amazed him to see blonde models on billboards in Latin American cities where almost everyone had dark hair. The girls were delighted when he responded in Spanish. Jim felt more comfortable with these girls than those he had just left in the States. Perhaps it was their virginity and naïve interest in him as an American. The two girls were truly crushed when they found hours and only by accident ran into another student from the center, but most of the time was devoted to study. Birú was elated at the time he had for books and progressed quickly. In the mornings he would study English. After lunch he would study with Peruvian teachers about his own country. But his favorite study was the movies about life in America.

Only the *campesinos* in California who picked the lettuce and the house builders worked in America. The idea amazed Birú but was confirmed by each movie. The rest drove tractors or sat in chairs and talked on the phone.

"God must love these people," he decided. "We work hard and have nothing. They do nothing and have miracles every day."

The months passed and Birú took to wearing the long pants and foreign shirts like the other students. After six months he could understand and speak English well enough to go the *cine* and not have to read all the subtitles to understand.

One day while sitting in the central plaza, two *gringo* hippies came up to him and tried to speak Spanish. Their Spanish was not up to it and he heard them say, "Let's find someone who speaks English."

"I speak," said Birú.

"Far out," they said and started speaking quickly.

"Hey man do you know a place we can crash. Not too expensive."

"Yeah," the other one said quickly. "Coke man where can we score some coca."

Birú felt ill. He could understand so little of what they had said. "You speak English?" he said, hoping by some mistake they were speaking another language.

"Sure man," the tall fair-haired one replied. "We're American." So this was his first encounter. *Americanos*.

"Do you know Washington, D.C.?" Birú asked.

They laughed good-naturedly and said, "Naw, man, we're from Marin."

"I go to Washington, D.C. in one week," Birú said.

"Far out!" the one with curly hair said.

"Yes, it is very far" Birú replied.

The two *gringos* laughed together.

Birú tried to answer their questions about the hotel. He told them that in the market they could find coca leaves.

"Say, do you know where we can exchange some money?" the blond one asked.

"At the bank," Birú said.

"No, we mean black market," the curly-haired one said. And seeing his blank stare laughed and said, "Let's boogie to that restaurant. So long man."

Birú had grown used to the din of the city and could now think privately surrounded by the noise of the cars. These men he had just talked to seemed drunk to him. They radiated a friendly festive spirit. They also seemed to be much less interested in him than he in them. Birú decided that when in America he must act *borracho*. He must greet strangers as old friends like he would do when drunk at the fiesta when he could not remember the names of men who were friends only the night before.

Birú wandered through the plaza looking at the people in front of his big hotel. He saw old *gringos* and their wives sitting in a bar drinking. He was anxious to go to their country and learn their ways. They were immensely strange to him but they were the ways of a people who seemed to walk on a golden bridge above the dirt road he had known. They were the ways of life where food and shelter, things that he had thought were a continual struggle, were seemingly given freely. The movies he had seen talked of work but the labors he had seen seemed easy and the rewards unending.

And what of these people drinking and looking for coca? His people needed coca to fight hunger and to work in the high *montañas.* Yet he knew these men did not need the coca to survive. Already at the center, his life seemed like one Sunday after another. Study was not work—this was pleasure.

Birú's mind swam with confusion. He had lived all his life at a level where to survive all those he knew had to work endlessly. This was what life had always meant to him—an endless struggle. Normal. There was the occasional drunk or cripple in the city who begged but that was also an endless struggle. Now he was surrounded by people who not only did little of any labor he would call work, but who were surrounded with tools that made their life even less laborious.

"They live in a Sunday world with their cars and machines," he thought. As much as my life has been of work, theirs is of pleasure. They all must know happiness that I cannot even dream of. In that sense then, Birú felt as the day approached for his departure that he was leaving for heaven there to be instructed by gods in the ways of ease and pleasure. I will learn their ways he thought and lift the terrible weight which pushes my *familia* and friends down so far into the sand that they cannot see these miracles. When I return I shall show them how to live.

7

The airplane roared and shook as it sped across the ground. People around him looked to have no great concern, but Birú thought he would soon be dead. Others from his training group appeared to share his concern. When the giant monster machine lifted into the air, Birú glanced over to see a *compañero's* face ashen—gripping the bars of his seat like the last thread of life. Soon they were miles in the air and the mountains looked like green breasts that jumped from a blue blanket fringed in white. *El océano,* he thought, I can see forever. Truly now I am with the gods. Below, he could see a brown path leading to a village no bigger than a dot. This is how the *norteamericanos* see the world, Birú thought. He imagined his family house, the hacienda, all small and pitiful from this perspective. My people know nothing of this, his thoughts continued, perhaps they hear a roar and see a white trail as I used to do. But I had no idea. To his right he saw out of the window, on the other side of the plane, mountains thrusting into the sky with their white caps. These are places no man goes, he thought.

The gentle passage through the air soon began to dull his early extreme fear. Instead he began to feel warm and secure, much as he remembered how it felt to be in his mother's arms.

Soon, as it had been happening regularly in the last six months, a feast appeared. A combination of meat, salads and sweets that he only would have formerly known on a high holiday or a wedding. From where it came he knew not, but always there was food for these *gringos*. Three times a day—meat. He did not understand how these people who hardly ever saw a cow could dine forever.

In the seat next to him sat an elder *gringo*. Birú glanced at his suit and tie of many colors. On the wrist of the man was a gold watch and on his finger was a ring with a stone in it. The man had a suitcase open in front of him and was shuffling through papers. He looked over to catch Birú's stare then looked down quickly and smiled. Birú smiled back and said "man" as the two *gringos* in the park had done to him.

The man looked perplexed and smiled back. "You going to bow –gat–tow?" he drew out a name.

Birú did not understand but smiled back. The man shot out his hand and Birú took it.

"Una names a Burt," the man said. "Nace cunt-tree Columbeah. Where ya from?"

Birú smiled helplessly and looked at the man before him.

"Eyes from Texsis ben down herea helpin these boogies wit do all. Damn these here thunda hads a dun. Good thing we helpin dem. But shit no soona ya gt em in a suit den they want to snag evera thing ya been bulden. Damn shame some times ya thinks its hardly worth it. If n they don nut steal it from ya plain they broke ya to death."

The man was quite animated, sipping now and then from a brown drink. At one point he said, "Let me buy ya a coke, son, dis here is a burr bun beat yooz a to young fur dat."

Though the youth hardly understood the man talking to him he did garner the fact that it was from his generosity that a coke was forthwith delivered to him. He thanked the man in his Spanish-slurred English. These were the first words he had spoken.

The man's mood seemed to change and as it had been before when encountering *gringos*, Birú felt uneasy that he could not hold up any end of a conversation. He therefore continued to smile at the man until the Texan, smelling of liquor, let out a hardy laugh.

"Say," he said, "where ya goin in the States?"

Birú understood the words 'you go' and said "I go to Washington, D.C."

"You got people there?" the man asked.

"I am part of a new exchange program," Birú continued the monologue he had learned at school.

"Ah, government. Hey good, good, fine, fine, heh-heh," the man said nervously.

Birú noted that the big *gringo* was growing more nervous and the man soon got up, and saying he was going to the bathroom, picked up his case and left the seat.

Birú felt embarrassed and a bit scared, the man had obviously moved on account of him. His thoughts slipped back to the deferential frame of mind he was used to as a *campesino*. I must not expect to be one with these people, he thought.

In truth, Burt had moved away because of the incessant smiling of the youth. Because of the youth's race, Burt felt superior, but modern mores demanded that one temper this superiority with a bit of "noblesse oblige." Burt thought of himself as being worldly and passed off the qualms he felt about his ill-mannered departure from the youth's side as a legitimate search for more interesting conversation. These thoughts flashed through his mind almost too fast to be conscious and he was moments later comfortably ensconced in a new seat.

The effect on Birú, however, was more than momentary as he still felt his confidence failing. What was he doing here in the sky with all these people who knew so much and he so little?

Birú was still in this frame of mind when the plane began to descend into Bogotá. Birú felt the plane falling and his thoughts lowered themselves even to an even further level of humbleness—that of one of fear and prostration before his God. "Santa María, get me out of here," he thought as the plane fell down into dark billowing ominous clouds, dropping toward the mountains, banked its wing and descended into the darkness. The engines changed pitch to a higher whine and there was a whirring sound as flaps were lowered. The dark forms swirled outside the window and suddenly Birú was in the depth of a sea of clouds. The experience for one who had rarely known rain was startling and mysterious. Moments later the plane descended below the clouds and Birú in his fear was further mystified by green rich fields spreading out in the greyness below. As the plane's speed decreased, beads of water ran over the outside of the windows. The plane rushed down toward the ground and Birú observed curtains of clouds descending right to the verdant fields below. He could now see houses, cars and roads.

The noises around him quickened as the earth approached.

Birú was terrified and just as the earth rushed up to the plane at a sickening pace, power lines shot under him and there appeared a large road before them on which the plane fell. Suddenly, there was a tremendous bounce and increase in the sound of the jets. At this point, Birú nearly fainted. He felt dizzy and was perspiring heavily in a cold damp manner that seemed to sympathize with the swirling grey and pelting rain, and it was with with a feeling of intense relief that Birú realized they were on the ground.

Outside in the rain, military and commercial jets and small planes with propellers were parked in various spots around the field. The jet in which he was seated now was moving at the pace of a car, its engines only a dull whine. Birú was still stunned as the jet came to a halt before a building. He sat there motionless as the cabin emptied around him.

The *gringo*, Dick Keating, came back to his seat. They now conversed in a slang combination of English and Spanish. Keating looked down at the young man. He had grown fond of Birú in the preceding six months. He felt that there was a faith and trust between them. But just as he felt the brotherly camaraderie, he also was prone to tease Birú as he would a younger brother.

"How ya doin' Birú?" he asked in their standard greeting.

Birú was startled, still dazed by the landing. Keating's smiling face comforted him, and together they went into the transit waiting area. There was a large duty-free store and through the glass partition Birú could see large crowds bustling about. Outside the rain had abated and he stepped out on a balcony set aside for viewing the field. A young newspaper vendor approached and asked if he wanted a paper and after receiving the negative asked Birú where he was going.

The newspaper boy was approximately Birú's size but lacked the bucolic vigor of Birú's face and eyes. He was more shallow, his eyes more piercing and cynical, yet there were similarities; they were both Indian and shared many physical characteristics.

Birú asked about the youth's life in Bogotá. He was fascinated to hear the youth's confession that he was actually a criminal.

"My friends and I steal the wallets," he said.

"And you don't get in trouble?" Birú asked.

"No, *compañero* it's easy, *muy fácil* and the people here have so much *plata*. One time the *norteamericanos* send down their best cop. He is a big *federale* from the F.B.I. So he comes here to teach our police how to catch pickpockets. I didn't know but I hear that this man got picked at the airport and I look at my haul for the day and there was the *federale's* wallet. Oh *chucha madre*, I laugh when I remember how easy it was to take that burro's wallet. Heh-heh."

He kept laughing in such an infectious manner that Birú soon joined him.

"*Sí, mi compañero*, it's a good life," he boasted. "I got a motorcycle and smoke the best *puente rojo mata*," he rolled his eyes up expressively, "and pure coca. I bet you grow it, don't you, *hermano?* You want a hit man? Want to see what we do to your leaves up here?"

With this he took out a small leather bag and with a short metal straw stuck up his nose, he took a tremendous snort. "Now you, *hermano*, try some," he said.

Birú looked with suspicion at the white crystals in the bag. "This is coca?" he questioned. "Coca is a leaf," he said inquiringly to his new friend.

"*Sí, campesino, mierda* this stuff is made from the leaf, idiot, why you'd have to chew a bushel to get this much cocaine. *Prueba un poco, amigo.*"

Birú inhaled as the youth had done and felt as if a damp paste had blown into his throat and nose. As he left the deck and the pickpocket, Birú checked to see if his wallet was still there and was embarrassed to find that it was.

The thief saw his actions and laughed. "Keep your wallet in your front pocket around here. *Adiós amigo, buen viaje.*"

Walking down the bustling hallway Birú began to feel detached. The sounds grew more hollow and his legs began to course with excitement. First he thought it was the anticipation of flying again, yet now instead of fearful he was excited and euphoric.

"*Madre vamos*-let's go" he thought "Coca at home to feel better not hungry, so you can breathe," his thoughts flashed in spurts like a well pump. Put, put, put faster and faster. "Powder like snow to get high, laugh, *ínga* eat leaves because they're high, *gringos* breathe powder like snow to get high, leaves, snow, high, poor, rich, jets." The roar of the planes on the field blended with the sounds in his head that continued even as Birú reentered the hollow cavity of the jet again. The cabin had a smell of burnt fuel, yet looked shiney and cleans.

The speed as the giant machine left the ground united into one with Birú's thoughts. Before he had felt alienated and fearful of the take-off from Lima, now the plane and he were one hurling into the sky. Raw power devouring space into the cavernous catacombs of his mind. Fear did not matter anymore. There was nothing that could stand before the power of his mind. Birú was eager to meet this beast, the United States, his legs tingled and his adrenaline flowed. He jumped out of his seat and started for the front of the plane. He could not sit still.

A stewardess stopped him and said that he must return to his seat.

He tried to push past. "I'll conquer you," he muttered.

The stewardess drew back and started to call for help.

Birú felt strong hands on his shoulders and turned to look into a smiling face of a young brown-haired *gringo*.

"Come sit with me, *amigo*," the *gringo* said in perfect Spanish.

"Careful," the stewardess said in English, "I think he's dangerous. A hijacker, I'm going to warn the captain, hold him."

The *gringo* muttered some disparaging remark that seemed to imply he'd like to see the Indian he was holding succeed. Just then Dick Keating came up and calmed the stewardess, explaining that Birú was quite harmless and was a guest of the United States government. He then turned and looked at Birú, curious at this strange outburst. "Do you want to sit with me?" he asked Birú in English.

"No, I'll sit with my new friend," Birú said with conviction in Spanish.

Keating turned away puzzled as the two of them walked away.

The *gringo* introduced himself as Jim Klondike and thereby

began a friendship that was to be perhaps the single greatest influence of Birú's multitudinous experiences in the United States.

Take the pipe JK

8

Jim Klondike had been born in the United States, raised in India, Nepal, Europe, and South America as the son of a doctor. His father, a genial and quiet man, had been a missionary and then a State Department doctor. Jim had had a unique exposure to the world. He had grown tall and strong and enjoyed an active and successful athletic bent. Like his father and mother Jim was handsome, mild-mannered, interested in many endeavors and enjoyed working at home on his own devices or in conjunction with some family project.

By the time Birú met him, Jim strongly felt the need for radical social change in the world, in revolution and violent reaction of the oppressed. Yet he thought himself weak and lacking in commitment because he had never personally taken up arms for the cause of justice. During the previous three years, he had lived and studied in Latin America and had spent a summer traveling by Land Rover throughout Africa. These experiences had led to his belief that the United States and Europe had been fundamentally corrupted by their rich, resource-sucking lifestyles. Perhaps it was the extreme sensitivity in Jim's own nature that made western opulence seem so repugnant when surrounded by the sea of poverty he knew the rest of the world to be.

In class at American University a young inexperienced classmate had tried to argue the case that America was providing so much technical and financial assistance to the "third world."

Jim, mild-mannered as ever and loath to make a spectacle of himself, raised his hand to make a rare comment.

"While I do not want to negate the *philanthropic* urges of the United States," he said with the slightest bit of sarcasm, "it seems abundantly clear to me that the history of man is characterized by men preying on men and nations. There are forces in our own present time that are working for the betterment of man, but far greater is the evidence of our country and our society devouring what it will, much as a salivatory wolf would a trapped flock of sheep. The differences between foreign aid and imperialism are at times quite hard for me to perceive."

By now Jim had given the longest public speech of his life and was growing increasingly nervous, but the tension in him cried to be released in any form. He forced himself to continue.

"Throughout the world, utilizing militaristic and economic means, the United States overtly and covertly supports subservient puppet governments and leaders that serve our economic interest far more than those people whom they would purport to represent."

Jim looked down as a profound silence filled the room. The professor smiled blandly and continued to lecture in the double talk that characterizes discussions of national security which was his topic. Jim, however, did not hear him as his ears burned red and adrenaline rushed through his body. His mind flashed back to scenes of poverty and Sisyphean labors he had observed by countless toilers throughout the world. He comforted himself by the thought that he would soon be away from this banality and corruption and back in Latin America where he had arranged to study a semester in Quito, Ecuador. At least I'll be back with people again—for as such he characterized the majority of the population of the world for which he felt such great compassion.

Jim walked to his bike through the bare trees of the early winter campus. As he rode down Nebraska Avenue with the cars whizzing by him he longed for the relative tranquility of the rest of the world. Again, he felt the bitter twang of anxiety stemming from the lack of ability to feel at home in his own country and, for the present at least, his inability to find a permanent home in a country better suited to his own temperament.

The family house was empty when he entered, stacked to the brim with mementos from many lands. His family was gone, his father and mother on temporary assignment in Tangiers, and his brothers and sister in various colleges. He packed a traveling backpack as he had done so many times before as the familiar anticipation and excitement welled up in him. An insight crossed his mind that perhaps he created on purpose his immense dissatisfaction on being home in the United States because he felt such great satisfaction and happiness when leaving. A friend had once told him of ideas that haunted the mind endlessly—problems that never led to solutions. "Well, for the time being," he thought, "I can just relax and enjoy what's happening."

Jim locked the house and left the key with a neighbor. A friend drove him to the airport where he was to catch a flight to Miami. Jim loved airports. There was an air of excitement and drama about them—lovers parting, soldiers on leave, businessmen. Jim walked through the electric doors of the terminal and into the red carpeted area. Two young college girls with their hair typically parted in the middle eyed him with friendly interest. He was hungry and searching too but the chance encounter, the act of the pickup, was beyond his emotional means.

He purchased his ticket and boarded the plane. After the takeoff, he went to sleep with the ease of one who has spent much time on airplanes. A stewardess awoke him once and gave him a sandwich, which he placed in his woven Colombian shoulder sack.

In Miami, he went to the Ecuatoriana Airlines ticket counter and, after showing his official red diplomatic passport that he got as the son of an American official, paid the fare. The Ecuatoriana flight was a prop and cheaper. But even if it had the same price as the American jet that provided the service to Quito, Jim would have taken the Ecuatoriana airline, preferring to be in something resembling a Latin American environment as soon as possible.

After a two hour wait spent people watching and reading the work of a leftist historian, Jim made his way down to the lower beat up part of the airport. There were no comfortable lounge chairs or television chairs to sit in. On a lone bench against the wall sat a fat brown-skinned man. "Mestizo," Jim thought, laughing at himself at how the man who was so well off in his country and lauded his fraction of white blood over the Indians, looked and felt so inconsequential in this citadel of white supremacy.

While standing in line for the plane, Jim watched two middle-aged middle-American types haggling with a steward about the loading of a big box marked TV.

"Young man," the officious older American said, "I have made this flight before and do not wish to risk this television in the hold."

"I am sorry, sir, if that goes, it goes in the hold," the attendant responded in slurred English.

Another five minutes of arguing and a bribe and the TV was successfully loaded in the cabin. The man and his wife, obviously pleased with themselves, caught Jim's stare. The man smiled and said, "Just got to know how to handle these things."

"You have some experience?" Jim interrogated dryly.

"Been down ten years. We're missionaries. LDS," the man said.

"In Ecuador?" Jim replied. He felt disgust and little respect for the missionaries, not so much for what they did, the school and radio stations had some benefits, but rather the sanctimonious holier-than-thou motives. Jim despised the way missionaries loathed to mingle with the people they were trying to help, living in compounds behind barbed wire. But his parents had been missionaries in India and he reflected on a missionary couple who had picked him up once hitchhiking in Colombia and taken him home to share a meal. In a grove of trees, these fine people had set up an orphanage where they would nurse malnourished infants and send them back to the States to foster homes. Jim had even given them some money, though they hadn't asked for it. He reflected further on the kindnesses shown to him by missionaries in Africa. It wasn't, he decided, their acts that were erroneous, it was the, "No you're doing it all wrong. My way is right" attitude. The government does the same thing, his thoughts continued, only their motives...

His thinking was interrupted by the smiling visage of the American lady. Jim blushed and smiled back in his natural way.

"Are you a Christian?" she asked softly.

"No, ma'am," Jim replied, though his thoughts were more along the lines of "Hell no!"

The answer triggered a response in the couple prompting them to go into an obviously much rehearsed missionary act.

"Son," the man said piously, addressing him as if he were a total idiot—another heathen Indian to be shown the light, "the Bible says that God gave his only begotten son to mankind that they might be saved. Do you believe in God, son?"

The whole scene was so bizarre at 3:00 a.m. that Jim momentarily had the urge to proselytize back at him about some guru a friend of his had been telling him about a few weeks before. "God is presently on Earth in the form of R Maharaj Chaiai Singh Ji and I am one of his apostles." As a compromise between his urge to be ludicrous or engage the missionary in what he knew would be a unreasonable theological debate, Jim replied to the question by saying he was an animus and thought God was energy and all the world a manifestation of that source.

The wife who had been holding back, letting her husband do the preaching, looked at Jim with pity and a hint of disgust.

"Son," the missionary said holding up his bible. "There is only one truth and that is written on these pages."

Mercifully the line began to move and Jim was able to separate himself from the missionaries' presence. "If there is a hell," he thought as he crossed at a crisp pace to the plane, "it would be to be trapped with the likes of that uncompromising ignorance for eternity."

The plane was an old D-4 turboprop affair and looked like it had seen better days. Jim sat down in his seat and arranged himself to sleep. He took his shoes off and while bending over saw a cockroach or beetle scurrying by his hand. Jim laughed, his spirits soaring at this sign of life. "Better than those other sterile tubes," he thought comparing this plane to the efficient hypergenic flight down from Washington to Miami.

Jim awoke a few hours later as the sun was rising over Central America. "Costa Rica," he thought. He reached into his bag and removed the sandwich he had gotten that night. He looked at his watch. It was 5:30 in the morning. They had been flying for over two hours. Below the Panama Canal swept underneath with its giant ships plying their way through the passage. The sight of the Canal prompted Jim to recall a conversation with a foreign service office friend of his family. The stately old gentlemen had been laughing at Panama's claims that they were not going to renew the lease on the Canal and were going to take over the operation themselves.

"Why," the old fellow had snorted bombastically, "even if we were to agree, the rest of the world would never stand for it. Colombia would invade within minutes. The Panamanians have no sense of maintenance. They'd destroy the Canal. The Latino lets things run down. All they are interested in is to garner as much profit as they can until the source is bled dry. Why they've killed out Jim was not staying and made him promise to call them when he returned.

"Looking to get married," Jim thought. They'd throw themselves at you with all that Latin fire. It was hard to refuse sometimes. Jim reflected on how being an American made him automatically rich in their eyes and how marriage to him would be a ticket to the United States. "It's hard to tell," he decided, "if they want you or if they want to go to that magic Disneyland where the streets are paved with gold and lined with dishwashing machines. Oh well, it's still flattering. An American stranger would never approach you like and they are so beautiful!"

After a forty-five minutes flight over green fertile mountains, the snow-capped peaks of the Andes began to appear. As the plane swung over the city of Quito, Jim observed the green patchwork of small fields stretching up the mountainsides on such a steep angle that they looked hard to walk across, much less farm. Through the hills ran valleys, behind which huge cloud-shrouded mountains jutted. Occasionally, the clouds would part revealing snow-capped volcanoes. Giant thunderheads rose above jungle carpeting both sides of the mountains. Jim drank in the verdant beauty of the country that sparkled like an emerald floating past the sun. At 9,500 feet and 40 kilometers from the equator the sun illuminated all that it touched with brightness that was startling.

Inside the airport, an American youth was complaining that his coat had been swiped. Small brown people short of stature but wide of chest due to the high altitude were everywhere. Jim moved with purpose through customs and refusing taxi service walked out into the street to catch a bus. On the road past the airport, cars from the newly enfranchised middle class drove by.

Jim stood in front of a nearly completed duplex. All around him the new, old and beautiful were merging. The city was building up quickly around hills where ancient fields were being farmed with newly acquired modern machines.

The buses that regularly rolled by were small and crowded with people. Jim attempted to board several but his pack and bag and size could not be accommodated on the vehicles. Rather than take a taxi, in deference to the high altitude and interesting sights, Jim walked for an hour slowly enjoying each step down Amazonas through the middle class business and residential area along the wide boulevard.

As in every big city in the world there were the familiar signs of American, European, and Japanese companies. It was from these citadels that commerce and resources were controlled and exploited. As Jim approached the center of the modern part of the city, whites began to appear. Also in evidence were mestizos, the Indians with white ancestors and the next on the ladder of social and economic hierarchy. In front of a fancy hotel, Indians sold rugs and curios to the rich tourists. The vast majority of the population were poor Indians who lived in rural poverty, most outside of the economy, trading their crops for other goods. The Indians selling the rugs struck Jim's attention. He recognized them as the famous Otavalos, the Jews of Ecuador. He had heard of these salesmen appearing all over the world to sell their beautiful products. Jim had seen them in Bogotá with their distinctive appearance of long black, braided hair, white calf-length pants, blue and plaid ponchos.

Jim stopped for some lunch at a small restaurant off the main drag. "Ah, a good beer," he thought, and ordered himself a pilsner. The bottle arrived, a big liter affair, which Jim greedily began to pour into a glass. He stopped the pouring at his usual level, liking a big head. "Ah shit," he thought as the beer kept flowing out of the glass like some eternal fountain. "Forgot about the altitude," he thought as he wiped up the beer.

A tall blond American, sporting a Fu Manchu moustache and Grateful Dead T-shirt came up the table.

"Got to watch that stuff," he said.

Jim smiled slightly up at the fellow. He did not want to deal with an American now, but the cat was friendly and his girlfriend pretty.

In the next few days, they all got to be good friends. Wally, or Walrus as he was called, had been passing though Quito when he was recruited by a local basketball team. He was now a local hero of sorts and loved to play the role of enfant terrible. He was like King Kong among the small Ecuadorians but unlike Kong, he enjoyed himself. One night, to Jim's great embarrassment, he got some Ecuadorian youths all mad by challenging the machismo. He bet them that they couldn't beat his girlfriend Suzanne at arm wrestling. Suzanne was athletic. She beat the youths; Wally started calling them "fags".

Jim tried to smooth things over but the Walrus kept egging them on. Finally he was bending over and running down the street squawking at them, "Chicken, *pollo*, *pollo*."

Jim hated him and felt like joining the Ecuadorians in beating his ass, but at the same time the sight of the Walrus jumping ass-backward down the street was hilarious. The Ecuadorians, however, failed to see the humorous aspects of the actions and started to move toward him threateningly. Wally turned around and glared at the Ecuadorians. For a moment it looked as if they were going to fall on each other and fight. Then Wally turned and went running away laughing. The Ecuadorians looked startled and then feeling braver jumped on a motor scooter and followed Wally at a safe distance, hooting at him. Wally could have destroyed them if they had gotten close enough to him but he took it all as a big joke.

After that incident Jim detached himself from the two Americans' company. As the days passed in the peaceful city, Jim's mind seemed to grow less cluttered and more capable of clearer thinking. Though his Spanish was adequate, he was less apt to talk. Likewise, the time he'd spent watching television and radio in the U.S. was filled with more immediate encounters with the vibrant life of the alien country. Jim began to feel that he could hear and understand better.

Soon school started. He made new friends, found a lover, and became interested in his classes. Society and self struck a comfortable balance.

One time Jim saw Wally again at a basketball game in the park. During a break Wally produced a Frisbee and Jim and he began to play on the grass. A crowd of Ecuadorians gathered. They were mostly country people who seemed to prefer the park to the streets when in the city. They were awed by the flight of the object and the catches. Jim felt embarrassed by it all and sat down. Another friend of his caught one between his legs and this brought the house down.

Two Ecuadorian youths chased a loose throw but were unable to catch it in the air. They tried to throw the Frisbee but were unable to make it fly straight, which made the device even more amazing in their eyes.

Observing the scene, Jim thought, "Even our toys are wondrous to these people." Again he was awed by the tremendous gulf that separated his and their culture. "How strange we are to each other," his thoughts continued. "How strange they are to me."

As much as he enjoyed Quito, Jim's trips to the countryside were the most interesting to him. The capital cities of the poor countries of the world are bastions of the elites. They are the most like the United States. It was humorous to Jim how North Americans would fly from one capital city to another and feel that they had experienced the country they had visited. Once while Jim and a friend were eating an avocado on a muddy street in a poor little village outside of Quito, a big air conditioned bus full of Americans pulled up. The driver and guide got out and went over and purchased some avocados for the people in the bus. A few of the most adventurous ones actually got off and stood around the bus. They looked so odd to Jim in their double knits and with their cameras. They hovered in these buses and fancy big hotels as if they were life support systems sustaining them on some strange uninhabitable planet.

Bill, a gregarious student from Wyoming, sauntered up to the bus and peered at the people like they were goldfish in an aquarium, laughing and pointing at different ones. The people in the bus smiled and laughed back. A few got out and talked to Jim and Bill.

They were fascinated and awed to find out that the two of them were hitchhiking. "It's great when you're young," one said, passing off his own lack of experiences on his older age.

Poverty in the big cities was more disturbing to Jim than what he experienced in the countryside. There most were poor and the contrasts did not seem so stark and depressing. There were not the hordes of begging children or the barefooted paupers shuffling by rich homes surrounded by high walls topped with broken glass to remind Jim of the eternal conflict of the society of man.

On the weekends Jim would flee Quito. Often he would go to a small town for market day. All the farmers and craftsmen from the surrounding countryside would gather to barter and trade any surplus they might have. Also in the market would be factory-made plastic and metal goods. In the bigger markets fine Indian crafts would be laid out for the tourists. The market would be a whirl of activity starting early in the morning and going until dark. Booths would act as stores and as Jim walked by fat brown ladies would shout out "*¡Para Usted caballero!*—For you, sir. Come see. *Mira*, look at my fine wares."

During the last part of his stay in Quito, Jim was encouraged to do a special study of a rural village. The professor recommended a small anomaly of a village of blacks in the middle of the Andes. While there were large populations of descendants of slaves on the northwest coast of Ecuador, the black Andean village of Chota was singular. Jim would go to the village on weekends, get drunk with the townspeople and listen to their stories. These people were the lowest social status, the untouchable, appreciated mostly for their contribution to the national soccer team. But they were very proud and happy in their village.

Jim was riding a local bus with one of the villagers and his son when a mestizo came up and demanded his seat. The black meekly started to rise. Jim stood up and having to stoop over in the small bus, looked down on the small man and said, "Here, pig, you can have my seat. I want this man, my friend, to be comfortable." Others around, who had been listening, laughed at the scene and Jim's words. The man looked like he wanted to apologize to Jim but turned away mumbling, "I did not know he was your friend."

"There is nothing distinctively American about racism," Jim thought. He did not like to impose his values, feeling as if he was a guest, but the black was his friend and Jim felt as if his point had been well taken even though he was now sorry he had called the man a pig.

When they returned to the village word got around of what Jim had done. That night Jim sat in the hut of the old lady, Mina, where he stayed and listened to her speak of her people. "We are not of these mountains. My mother's mother told me of our way before we were taken from the coast. My son will journey there maybe. We grow sugar and fruit here but," she laughed, "I don't like fruit."

Jim told her about Alonso de Illescas, an escaped slave who ruled the Zambo Republic, an area that stretched from Esmeralda to Colombia. She was fascinated by this history. From then on Jim could not return to the village without telling tales of this black warrior who had defeated all Spanish military expeditions sent to defeat him. He renounced the Catholic god and king, saying that "God is a god of freedom, god of life, which is beyond human empires, churches."

Jim sat there patiently, trying to understand the old woman's broken Spanish. Another member of the household came and said, "Enough, old woman. Jim is our champion. He does not want to hear your old tales. Come, *amigo*, we go drink the *aguardiente*."

At the mention of the word, Jim's insides convulsed. The drink was the local moonshine and was loosely translated "fire water". Strangely, Jim liked the stuff, though it was still a hard drink to get down. Jim walked over to another shack where a kerosene lantern was hung over the doorway. The room was full of strong laborers already drunk and in fine spirits. Jim's entrance into the room prompted a round of back slapping and greetings. "*Amigo, amigo*, drink!" A bottle was thrust into Jim's hand. The room was full of the pungent odor of sweat and the ether smell of the harsh alcohol. Jim took a sip of the beverage and gagged at first at the smell. The drink burned in his throat and his eyes began to water. Soon a pleasant warmth spread across his chest and he began to smile, feeling good about where he was and who he was with. He felt a great companionship between himself and those in the room. Occasionally the stuffy room would be convulsed in laughter. Jim would be irresistibly drawn into the laughter though he often had no idea of what the joke was.

"Jaime," a stocky man said drunkenly, "You are the only *blanco* that's my friend. *Los otros* come in cars to the *fábrica.* Tell me, *amigo*, how can I get a car?"

Another heard him and laughed aloud. "Anibal wants a car!"

The room filled with laughter and Anibal smiled along.

"*Sí*, I want a car. I want to go from here to the city and I stay with my friend Jaime," he said slapping Jim on the back.

There was more talk of Anibal's car, but then the conversation got stuck for a long time on the problem of a she-goat that was not giving milk. "You sure your goat doesn't have balls?" someone asked. "Ulises there killed his rooster because it didn't lay no eggs." The room broke up at the joke. Ulises grabbed a guitar and began to sing a song about a burro who thought he was a horse.

Jim wandered outside and sat under a tree by the river. The village was dark. Occasionally, a faint light from a candle would shine through the boarded slats of a shack. Jim looked at the stars. The farther south he got the more symmetrical the stars seemed. It was as if you could connect the dots to form bigger stars, triangles, rocketships or anything. He followed Orion to where it was dropping down to the horizon and the mountains. Below the dark forested slopes, the river meandered along. On both sides of the river were fields. A quarter of a mile down river was a single bright light marking the large buildings of the textile factory. Jim smiled on the form benignly. "That factory should belong to these people," he thought. "They should seize it." His thoughts ran through the old forms, the feeling of helpless anger over the injustices coursing through his mind like a practiced and boring rhyme, an old devil of a thought not to be exorcised by solution, only to be smiled on helplessly. "These people could seize it with their own bodies. But the government would come with guns. Money protects money. Only the rich can afford to buy arms. And who sells the best arms?"

Suddenly, he arrested his own thoughts. "Why do I worry? Stop it!" he said to himself. "I sit in the midst of beauty and agonize over the lot of man. There is nothing I can do about it. Enjoy the beauty," he counseled himself. "The Earth, the energy will go on when this is passed. *You can't change the world,* his grandfather had told him. You can't change the world, only experience and accept." The words fell through his mind like a tin can falling down a mountainside, hollow and twanging decibels descending into silence.

Jim's time in Quito was passing quickly. Toward the end of the term, Jim received a letter that heralded the arrival of Zach Taylor, an old and zany friend from Europe who was soon coming through Quito on his way to visit another mutual friend now living in Argentina. Jim had similar plans but planned to travel alone. Trepidation arose at the thought of traveling with Zach in South America.

Jim's stay in South America had changed him for the better, he thought. Instead of the confused escapism with which he had fled Washington, he felt more centered, at peace with himself. Now the insanity, the enjoyable insanity of Zach was approaching.

In many ways he and Zach were opposites. As serious as Jim would attempt to be in all his affairs, Zach was lighthearted and rebellious. At times it almost seemed they played off each other like black and white. They were both good looking and appealing to women. However, Jim's attitude toward the subject was to wait and approach a liaison cautiously. Zach, as he had seen him do many times would run in and out of a relationship in a week.

Zach likewise had a brilliant capacity in word and action to make any situation absurd. The effect of his friend could on occasion be stunning, leaving Jim not sure if he had really allowed himself to be led astray by such a maniac.

One time, Zach had called Jim in Washington, D.C. and invited him out to Virginia for tennis. Jim had arrived and as usual Zach was nowhere near ready. Finally, the two left for the public courts to find every one of them in use.

"J.K." Zach had said, "what a fool I've been. We can go play at these friends of the family. They've got this court next to a pool."

"You know them yourself?" Jim asked suspiciously.

"Yeah, sure," Zach had said.

Up the two of them drove to this high-posted gate and down a long driveway through manicured lawns. At one point Zach asked Jim to stop. Zach leaned out the window and asked a gardener, "Say, pard, which way to the courts?"

The old black man smiled and pointed toward a willow hedge.

Jim asked, "How come you don't know where the courts are?"

"Ain't been here in a while, J.K.. Ah, there they are. I don't think we need to ask. Let's start. Wait a minute." He again addressed the grey-haired gardener. "Say, are the Pearsons home?"

"No," the man said, "No Pearson here, only Adams. Mr. Luke Adams."

"You don't know their names!" Jim exclaimed. "Come on, let's split."

"J, J.K.," Zach said drawing the "K" out in a long sigh. "It's cool, man. I'm just bad with names, you know that."

After two close sets and a swim, the two were preparing to leave. Zach had walked off behind a bush to retrieve a ball and Jim was putting his shirt on.

Jim turned around to find an angry red visage peering at him over a hedge.

"Who may I ask are you?" the man whom Jim was certain was the owner of the estate asked.

Jim blinked dumbfounded and started to sputter an exclamation, expecting to be in jail by nightfall. At that moment Zach came scooting by, hand extended.

"Mr. Adams!" he exclaimed. "Zach Taylor, " he slurred his name. "You remember, Nancy's son? Brought Jim over to meet you. He's a pro, teaches tennis. I told him how good you were and he wants to take you on. Right, Jim?" Zach asked, slapping him on the back.

Jim just blinked, amazed at the effrontery of Zach's bold-faced lies.

"Well," Mr. Adams said. "I really can't today, but come back Monday afternoon. We'll have a go at it."

"Right," Zach said. "Well, we got to go. Thanks for the hospitality. So long."

"My regards to your mother," Mr. Taylor shouted after them as they sauntered away. "And ask next time if you want to use the courts."

Jim followed Zach and fought an urge to flee at a dead run.

With a final turn and a goodbye wave, Zack muttered, "It's cool, J. It's cool."

"Does he really know your mother, Zach?" Jim asked.

"Sure man, everybody knows Mom, you know that," Zach said, broke into an uproarious laugh and held up his upturned palm for a soul-slap from Jim.

Needless to say, the two did not return on Monday.

The day of Zach's designated arrival came and went. Upon returning from a quick trip to Bogotá two weeks later, Jim found a note at the school that read, *J.K.—Have arrived, am presently domiciled at the Hilton, Pensión Hilton, that is and anxiously awaiting our rendez-vous and sweet, sweet reunion. Love. Z Taylor.*

Jim hurried over to the pensión, a little cheap hotel in the new part of the city. After inquiring at the front for Zach, a brown-curly-haired fellow turned around and asked.

"Hey are you J.K.?"

"The same," Jim said.

"Well, I'm Jeremiah and I'm traveling with Zach. He's upstairs in the penthouse."

"The penthouse?" Jim inquired.

"Yeah, you'll see. Come on. He'll be glad to see you."

"Jim and Jeremiah walked up rickety steps. Outside the window Jim could see a cornfield with a clothesline running next to it. He could hear chickens clucking. On the roof of the building a dome tent was pitched. Zach was sitting and writing in the sun. At the sight of Jim he jumped up and hugged him.

"J.K., ol buddy!" he said, obviously exalted at the sight of Jim. "Been some time, man."

Jim laughed and said in a kind of Amos and Andy affectation he adopted occasionally with Zach. "Now Z, I know yas glad to see me but yas gonna be even gladder when ya see what I go for my ol' friend Zach. Some of Colombo's best weed."

"Oh yeah," said Jeremiah, whose eyes twinkled all the time, but when happy or excited looked like two bright moon glimmers. At that moment his eyes were at full moon capacity.

"Jim," Zach said. "This here is my good buddy and travelling companion Jeremiah Gold or known as Oro in these parts. Now shake hands and come out rollin'."

They spent the afternoon and early evening smoking, talking, and listening to Zach play guitar on the roof. The green hills were lit with bright Ecuadorian sunlight.

"Damn, Jim, I can't believe I'm here. This is incredible," Zach said. "Let's go walk around."

They left the hotel in the dusk light onto a residential street and headed for the main street of the city. On one corner an old Indian woman with a bright but dirty shawl stooped over a blanket of avocados she was selling for a penny each. The lines on her face stood out like water draining through mud. They passed a cathedral where other old women hovered in or around the doors. A gang of shoeshine boys descended on them like seagulls falling on a beached shark. Interspersed were beggars, little children who came up, hands extended, heads tilted up with brown eyes pleading, then after they got a coin, they would go running off, laughing. It was worth it to see those eyes bloom like a spring daisy in time-lapse.

On the main thoroughfare the rush hour traffic strained and groaned. As the trio approached the old part of the city, the streets got narrow and the buildings more rickety. "Man, these people are too fuckin' much. They live here?" Zach asked.

"Some do. Most stay in the country and other cities and come to trade," Jim said. "Now, gentlemen, some *ceviche de camerón.*"

The three ducked into a small restaurant. The walls were green and dirty. There were three small tables.

"Is it cool to eat anything I want?" Zach asked.

"Watch uncooked vegetables and the water," Jim said. "I eat everything. But I've got amoebas." With that Jim let out a giant sulphur burp to prove his point. The stench blew across the table.

"Sweet," Jeremiah said.

"Remember those basketball games after lunch in Vienna?" Zach asked and let out a big burp of his own.

After the beer and *ceviche*, a mixture of small shrimp, onions and vinegar sauce served with toasted corn kernels, the three walked through an open square. On each side were narrow streets with small stores and restaurants. A bus was preparing to leave for Ambato. Indians in bright red ponchos and hats with children in miniature versions of the attire stood on a corner by the bus. Short muscular men shouted and heaved bundles to be packed on the roof.

"This is where I usually eat," Jim said, gesturing to the middle of the square. Women sat in front of open baskets of cooked corn, eggs, pork, or soup. "You get a whole meal here for pennies."

The group returned to the hotel and smoked some more.

"What's going on with the band?" Jim asked Zach.

"Well I got laid off in Houston, but it's paying for this trip."

"What happened?"

"We were playing the Astrodome. You could hear notes played a minute after they were played bouncing all around the place. The stage monitors were all fucked up. I got the blame. But it wasn't all bad. I was pretty down backstage when this real slinker comes up to me with glitter on the eyes. We got to talking and she kept looking at me with them big bedroom eyes."

Zach was now in complete control of his audience and leading them down a pleasant erotic path. Jim knew that while there was undoubtedly a modicum of truth from whence this sprouted, it was liberally fertilized with bullshit.

"So," she says. "I hate to think of you staying at a hotel. You can crash at my place. So, I'm thinkin' hell yeah! I give her a little kiss and damn if she doesn't slip me a bit of tongue and grind. So, I say honey we're gone. We drive to her place and it turns out to be her parents who are out of town. Her grandfather sittin' on the wall with big horns over him. Crazy! We're on this woolly rug kissen and I slip my hand into her panties. And shit fire boys that lady was drippen and I was slippen. Turns out she's been goin to some women's college and was hornier than shit. We got it on <u>all</u> night long. She's still wiggling. Wouldn't mind seeing her right now."

Jim laughed and said, "Speaking of which, there are a few ladies who are anxiously awaiting our company. Carol, my old lady, has rounded up some friends to meet my rock star buddy."

Zach stuck out his hiking boots on the floor and said, "Did you tell them I was only a roadie?"

"No, only that you just got off tour."

Zach smiled. "Bullshit away!"

9

Two days later Zach awoke at first light. The girl that Jim had introduced him to lay sleeping beside him. Alice interested him. She had shown him around Quito and outlying towns. At the markets they had shopped for belts and shirts. "Don't keep your wallet in your back pocket," she warned.

Zach responded in an overdone Hindu accent, "It's cool, mama, this wallet has a special karma-backed guarantee. It's blessed by guru Swamaimommi."

"Well it's gonna need some heavy vibes in Latin America, especially Colombia," she laughed.

"How long you planning on being down here?" Zach asked.

"Long as the money holds out," she said with a peculiar timbre in her voice. "Anyplace is better'n the U.S.."

Zach had heard that tone before while living in Europe. It was strange to him. Every country had its own charm. Zach found the U.S. overwhelming sometimes with all its modernness, but at the same time he loved the challenges and games others detested and feared. He also had a seemingly unique hunger among his friends of wanting to be famous. Fame is what had drawn Zach to the outskirts of rock and roll as a roadie. He wanted to be a star, to be recognized in a crowd, and have beautiful women want to sleep with him just because of his fame. In the U.S. others might live in strangling numbers and confused alienation, but the famous were elites and lived in small villages with other famous—a village where everyone recognized you and knew all about you.

Politics attracted Zach. It was here where living in the limelight was the greatest challenge. Rock and roll was happening now. Robber Baron, sheiks' tables with his ambassador father, North Africa, presidential inaugurations, ideas and experience flashed through Zach's mind. Stoned on good dope, he was wired for thought. Good ol' stone energy rushes. Those ideas just fly by, watchin' the river flow. Get up for a five o'clock train. The idea stuck in his mind while other thoughts flowed by like a river around a sandbar.

Zach awoke. Outside there was some stirring about. Zach woke the others. He did not feel tired. "Save that for the train," he thought.

The three walked out into the dark. There was a bright light outside the hotel. They followed a cobblestone street. "The oldest street in Quito," Jim mumbled, glancing toward a small cavity of darkness on their right. A drunk Indian stumbled by, attempting to sing. He wore a ragged old Panama hat, calf-length pants, and a dark poncho.

"Hey, *gringo*," he cried slightly derisively.

"Hey *campesino*," Jim retorted.

"Hee, hee," he chortled off.

In a plaza, buses were lined up and crowds of Indians milled about in the dark. Others slept under the overhanging roofs.

The bus rumbled over the cobblestones.

At the station, ten people, obviously tourists, waited for the train. There was a young French couple that decided since they couldn't sit together to take the other train in two days. The train was actually a bus converted for use on the tracks. The *autocarril* pulled out into the dawn through the poorest part of Quito. Shacks were scattered down the hillside as the train climbed above them. Below, a small girl in a torn tab dress tried to pick her way through a mephitic sewer behind her shack. The *autocarril* zigged out of the valley of Quito and into the mountains past villages with African type grass huts. At one point the grade was so steep the train had to go down a section backwards. In this manner it zigzagged down toward the jungle.

Zach slept a little and watched the scenery. There was a free seat at the front of the train. Zach moved up and sat down next a conservative looking American dressed in a suit and tie.

"Mind if I sit here?" Zach drawled.

The man smiled at Zach meekly. He was light of stature, balding and wore glasses.

"This is some train, heh? More like a bus I'd say."

"It is a bus actually," the man said. "A bus on tracks."

Zach smiled at the man benignly. "Where are you from?" he asked.

"New York. I came to ride the train."

"Are you interested in trains?"

"I've ridden in trains all over the world."

The man was an accountant and spent his vacations each year riding on trains. "Next year it's the Trans-Siberian."

Across the aisle a young couple not much older than Zach were eating out of a box lunch.

"Where did you get that?" Zach asked. "I didn't think there was a ham sandwich to be had in a thousand miles of here."

The young man , handsome but soft, smiled and explained, "The hotel made them for us. We're on a tour. Tomorrow we're flying back to New York."

Zach suddenly felt that he had been through all this before—a dejà vu. It was odd like everything had an echo. He was going to tell them of his own experiences traveling and touring. The echoing, the thought crossed his mind to listen not talk. The part of his mind speaking to him was that which lectures. The lecture in his mind was not to be restimulated. Listen when someone is talking to you. Don't be thinking of your own related experiences.

Zach sat back in his seat. The mirror above the driver reflected the tits of the girl across the aisle. If he was a rock and roll star, the girls would come to him, even down here. All he had was his charm. Some people worry about it all the time, always wanting a boyfriend or girlfriend. You just got to let it happen.

The train was in the jungle now. The people were black and larger than those in the mountains. In the evening the train pulled into a station across the river from Guayaquil. Boys ran up to try to carry their bags and others to see what they could steal. The air was hot and humidity clung to the skin like a damp cloth. A boat brought the passengers across the wide dank river. Zach watched debris float by.

"I don't know about you boys," Jeremiah said, "but this city is going to have a hard time holding me to its bosom. Man, it's hot."

"I'm for splitting," Jim said. "Just a big city."

The three walked into a hotel. The front desk was in a wide patio on the second floor. A fan whirred on the ceiling. After a shower they waked down a wide boulevard to the water's edge, sat on the bank and watched rats scurry about the rocks. On the way back to the hotel a gang of barefooted children ran up begging. Zach took out a bunch of change and handed it to one. In with coins was a bill. There was screaming and shouting as the youths wrestled for the bill.

"Hey, hey," Zach said. "Divvy it up but don't fight."

"Shit, Zach," Jim laughed. "You gave them five dollars. That's a lot of jack."

By that time the dispute had been settled and the youths were running and playing around the street.

"They don't have it so bad," Zach thought, seeing how much the young beggars used the streets for their games.

The next morning after several faulty instructions, a bus was found. As the soon as the bus left the city, the paved roads ended. The bus followed a dirt track back up into the mountains and south. Jim had wisely advised everyone to sit at the front of the bus in order to have more leg room. A drunk man stumbled down the aisle and blew his lunch out the window. The bus was old and small as were most of the means of public transportation in South America.

Jeremy took out a kazoo and mouth harp. With Zach singing and playing guitar, the two launched into a rendition of Rocky Raccoon. The *campesinos* on the bus could hardly hear the broken notes but when Zach glanced back, he saw only smiles on the brown

Jolly holding it in

tanned faces.

Cuenca was a small town on the banks of a fast flowing river. The bus arrived at night. Jeremiah watched apprehensively as their backpacks were thrown down off the roof. The streets were cobblestone and laid out over the hills that ran down to the riverside. The three found a hotel in a square next to the market. The room was on the second floor, the first floor taken up by a narrow hallway. On the right side of the hallway was a small restaurant. The room contained three cots and opened to a small balcony that overlooked the square.

As the three were preparing to leave the room in the morning, there was the sound of an accident outside. The three crowded on the balcony and looked down on the people converging from every corner on the square. A military truck had run into a bus.

"Looks like the biggest thing that's happened in this town since the conquistadores," Zach laughed.

Also on the balcony was a young American woman.

"Fuck the accident," Zach thought. "Pretty exciting," he said smiling over at the girl. She reminded him of an old high school girlfriend.

The girl smiled back and asked where they were coming from.

Jeremiah suggested that they all go to the market and get some fruit for breakfast.

"I'll get my friends and meet you downstairs," the girl said.

Her friends were two other girls..

"What are you doing down here" Zach asked.

"We all go to Antioch College and we're traveling around for credit. By the way, my name is Toni and this is Trish and Pam.

"Howdy ladies," Zach doffed his cap, a floppy sports car hat with a wide brim.

"You're getting credit for this?" Jim asked incredulously.

"Yeah, we're supposed to be learning Spanish."

"It's a rip-off," Trish the girl from the balcony said. "We pay them $3,000 for tuition and they give us $800 to travel. You do the math. Do you guys go to school?"

"Jim and I do," Jeremiah said. "Zach works for Raz."

"The band?"

"Used to," Zach mumbled.

"Far out. I saw them once in Chicago. Good show. What are you doing down here?"

"Vacation. The band is taking a break, writing some new tunes. As a matter of fact, I'm going to finish up college after this."

"What the hell for?" Toni asked. "You got a great job. What do you want to go to college for?"

"It's not the degree, just the education, man. There's a lot of things I want to learn."

Zach glanced at Jim to see if he was enjoying his bullshit, knowing that Jim was as studious as Zach was lackadaisical. When they were in high school together sharing the same small classes at the American International School in Vienna, Zach would often be tardy due to an internal clock that kept him up late at night.

He was always learning, but it wasn't in any school. In high school it seemed at times that he was interested in anything else but the information the teachers were trying so ardently to impart.

He'd been good in history, but had, typical for him, incurred the unending wrath of the teacher by his continual pranks. One time, when the class had been at their desks in a horseshoe around the lecturing teacher, Zach had started a bet circulating that he could hit Rhonda Jenkins sitting at the far end with a spitwad. Not only hit her, but hit one of her small but freely given breasts. Zach let fly with the wad just as the news of the impending event reached the ears of Jenkins. She turned in shock to meet the cud as it struck its appointed spot. Her screams mingled with the spontaneous applause and discussion that erupted upon impact. The teacher was less than pleased, and conferred upon the malefactor a much lower grade than he deserved for academic reasons at the end of the semester. It was not that Zach was lazy or indolent. He merely focused most of his large amount of innate energy toward his two loves—music and women.

Zach had made an impression on the small school by forming a band and playing at the first dance of the year in the high school cafeteria. He'd moved on to playing night clubs in Vienna and had missed part of their senior year while he toured Europe with a band. Zach was good enough to be a star but the closest he'd ever gotten to the big time was working for Raz, a band he'd met while they were on a European tour.

Nobody seemed to care that the music was good. From backstage one could not see and barely hear the band. Zach had loved the scene, like a club with better looking girls, and had joined the crew to set up and take down the equipment. Being a roadie was all right, better than college. While the band was playing, the roadies had first crack at the girls that had gotten backstage in hopes of getting closer to Raz.

The memory of supple young bodies excited Zach as did the endless possibilities of sleeping with girls whose names he couldn't remember. Sex and girls were a common topic amongst the three boys.

As they were walking up the stairs by the river in Cuenca, Zach said, "Now take Trish. Did you hear her talking about her liberated sex life in college? Everybody sleeping with everybody's former lover. Positively incestuous, confusing as hell it would be. Give me true love or free but spare me, please, all that confusion in between. What about you? Were you sorry to leave Carol in Quito? You seemed quite happy together."

"We were," Jim said. "I'll be seeing her again in September in New Mexico. I don't know, it's hard for me to stay with a woman. I get attached to them and they to me and I always end up splitting. It's like I've got this defense now that limits me from reaching out. Like Carol made all the moves. It's lucky I get together with anyone at all."

"That's why they call it getting lucky."

Jim laughed. "Think you'll ever settle down?"

"No seriously. I don't know if you'll believe me but at times it gets to be like sports. Like you get in a pickup game of basketball with a bunch of strangers and have a great time. You feel good, like everyone, smile and laugh, say good-bye. It's the same wham-bam thank you ma'am."

"Do you ever fall in love?" Jim asked quietly.

"All the time. But it comes and goes. I'm getting better at avoiding those big highs and lows," Zach said.

"What you mean?"

"A general principle—as high as you get you'll drop down as low. I've got it so I go a little down a little hopefully getting a little higher each time. But every once in a while it's just too good and I know that I'm in for a big fall—that I'm going to eat it."

Oro and the pipe

10

The Americans were at the Peruvian border arguing with a guard that they did not want to buy a bus ticket out of Peru. "We want to take the boat over Lago Titicaca," Jim repeated for the fifth time. For hours they argued in the hot room where the officials sat at their desks. A women came in carrying pots of food for the guards. Along a wall sat a nun, some families of undetermined nationality waiting for some undetermined event. Zach was sitting with the pack and strumming on his guitar. In the midday heat he picked a traveling blues. He started to sing and thus began an epic verse that grew with each successive bummer.

By the time the argument had been settled all were in possession of much inflated bus tickets out of Peru and into Bolivia, and it was too late to catch the bus to Lima. Zach was trying to talk Trish into temporarily leaving the group and hitchhiking to Lima.

At the moment it was clear that Zach was focusing his primary interest in the direction of Trish Taylor. Jim looked at the girl and understood Zach's interest. She was pretty and strong. Her long blonde hair hung freely behind her back and her full breasts hung freely beneath a colorful Guatemalan shirt. The look she affected was typical, even mundane in the United States, but in northern

Peru the sight was positively devastating. With her at his side, Jim knew they would have no trouble getting a ride.

Jim lacked Zach's flair for conversation. He was so terrified of being rejected that he rarely if ever reached out.

Zach had always been amused by the situation of men and women longing for each other but "terrified to take the chance" as he had written in one of his songs. "When searching eyes land on you, respond, get through the fear."

Jim had seen Zach cause pain by breaking through an emotional barrier only to realize the woman's reason for having the barrier by not become the eternal lover of her dreams. He watched as Zach charmed Trish with his humor and wit. They were sitting on a park bench in the desert town of Tumbes. Schoolgirls passed, stared and giggled at Jim and Jeremiah. Trish appeared to be amused but not enchanted. She looked up once and caught Jim's stare and smiled prettily. Jim felt a surge of energy and blushed.

"C'mon Oro, let's walk," he said, wanting to get away. Nothing had been said. Women often smiled at him. Here was something different. Something he did not understand. It seemed as if he had walked around the bend into the arms of an old friend, yet they had never met before. Still it was like he'd seen that smile a thousand times before. The feeling was uncanny and disturbed him.

Jim and Jeremiah left the others and walked down a street past walls painted with revolutionary slogans. Jeremiah who had been trying to chat it up with the local girls via his limited Spanish or Berlitz smiled and said "hola" to a passing woman. The woman turned toward them and Jeremiah asked, "*¿Dónde está catederal?*"

which he knew perfectly well was right in front of them looking like every other cathedral in Latin America, an overdone, gilded testament to the power and glory of the Catholic Church.

"It's right there," the woman said. "You're American?" She asked in English. She was middle-aged and attractive, with a wide smiling face and seemed amused at Jeremiah who was so obviously trying to pick her up. She agreed to go with them into a small cafe for a drink. They sat beneath palms in a courtyard and ordered beer.

Daniela quickly opened up to them. "I live on a farm with my husband. If anyone sees me with you, I'll be in trouble." She laughed, waving her hand toward the street from which they were in plain view. She went on to describe the role of women in Peruvian society as being either whore or mother. She herself said that she had graduated from the university and had a professor for a lover. "All the other girls in the university seemed to be there to get a husband rather than a degree. The men want this too. I've two daughters who already are attracting serenades under their window."

"Yes," Jeremiah said. "We saw one of those. Zach and I were walking around looking for some entertainment."

Jim had already heard the unedited version of the story. The two had been looking for a whorehouse.

Jeremiah continued, "When we saw these guys we listened to their beautiful music. So they ask us if we play and ol' Zach, who is a pretty good musician, takes one of the guitars and starts playing some Bach with everyone nodding approvingly. The Bach somehow slides into a rock and roll progression and there's shock on the faces of the *rondallas.* They grabbed the guitar back. They liked it before he started playing that boogie."

The lady laughed. Two pretty teenaged girls came up to the table. They were fashionably dressed with slacks that came up above their waists that gave their backsides a long drawn out look.

The lady introduced them as her daughters and perhaps to cover for why she was sitting with two young men, suggested that the two girls show them around the town. Just then Zach, Trish and the other girls from Antioch showed up. Somehow Jim was left with the mother and American girls while Zach and Jeremiah went for a walk with the daughters.

"You must excuse me," the mother said. "I must follow at a discreet distance. We are still after all a conservative society."

Jim and the girls left with the mother to act as chaperones of Zach and Jeremiah and her daughters.

Jim was acutely aware of Trish walking beside him, but didn't say anything. She smiled up at him. "You've lived all over the world. That's really great."

Jim nodded, but did not say anything.

"Where did you like best?" the girl kept on talking and asking questions. Jim could feel that she wanted him. He was flustered at first but as the evening passed and he saw he was not mistaken, his confidence grew.

The next morning he and Trish sat beside each other on the bus and if Zach was concerned at having been rejected he didn't show it, and had switched his attention to the other two girls.

The bus ride to Lima was uncomfortable but Jim barely seemed to notice the twenty-four hours along the barren wasteland of coastal Peru as they shared the details of their lives. She had a high chuckling laugh that encouraged him to tell humorous stories, many of which involved Zach and his antics. He was adept at sleeping on buses. He gave her the window seat and suggested she use her coat as a pillow. But she ended up leaning against him and he stayed awake most of the night with the pleasant sensation of her head resting against his shoulder.

They reached Lima early in the morning and used the phone at the bus station to try and find a friend of theirs from high school. Manny's father had been the ambassador to Austria from Peru. His family was one of the oldest and most distinguished in the country. He lived in Miraflores, the part of the city inhabited by the wealthy elites. Manny was a drummer and had played with Zach. They couldn't find him in a phone book, but called an office listed under the family name and left a message.

The next stop was as always when first arriving in a major city, the American Express to get mail that had been sent by their families.

Here, Jim found a message to call home immediately.

Suddenly, his carefree traveling days and courtship of Trish was over. The news was bad. His father had cancer and was not expected to live long.

The mood was somber in the group as Jim made arrangements to catch the next flight to Miami and then D.C..

If he had any doubts that Trish cared for him it was dispelled by her coming with him to the airport where she held his hand at the gate and with tears in her eyes said that she would write and wanted to see him soon.

As the jet climbed into the sky and headed north, Jim felt that everything had changed, that he had rounded a corner, and his life as an adult lay before him. His thoughts were interrupted by an Indian who was causing a problem on the plane.

Before thinking about the consequences, Jim was up and talking to the *campesino*. Perhaps it was relief to have one more contact with that he had left, so after Jim calmed the man down, he sat with him.

They changed planes together in Miami and by the time Jim and Birú reached Washington, D.C., they were good friends and Jim had begun the many long conversations they would have on what could be done to right the long history of injustices to the indigenous populations of Peru and Latin America.

11

Forty years later Birú still remembered sitting on that jet plane with Jim. Maybe it was because all his senses had been opened wide, pried apart by clawing hands of stimulations, part *coca* that he had foolishly accepted from the pickpocket in the Bogotá airport and part amazement at all that was happening to him. By the time they had changed planes in Miami and were actually in the United States heading for Washington, D.C. Birú's mind was ready to listen to his new friend speak openly of what was only whispered of at home.

"The *inga...*" Jim had used the term with which they called themselves, "must fully join and participate in the political and economic life of the country or there will be no country. The days of subjugation and domination of the indigenous people by their colonial masters must end."

"But how?" Birú had thought but said nothing and continued to listen.

Once in Washington with others who had been taken from the fields to learn the ways of the modern world, Birú heard more talk of the rights of indigenous people—not so much from the other students in the Person to Person Corps program but from their teachers and other *americanos* like Jim who spoke of democracy and human rights.

After training for six months at George Washington University, Birú was sent to work at the Organization of American States in the beautiful marble Pan American Union building next to the White House. Here, first with so much awe he could hardly speak, Birú was shown into a luxurious office that spoke of power and importance to meet with *señor* José Miguel Insulza Cabrera, the deputy director of the O.A.S.

There had been nothing in the *bildalgo's* manner of speaking to him of the Vaati's, the *bacendado* from home, who thought no more of his *campesinos* than he would his other animals. *Señor* Cabrera spoke in a beautiful exotic-sounding Spanish of the upper classes of Argentina, almost like another language. "You are here to learn, but also to teach. We want you to be there when we speak of the issues relating to the rural poor, *los indios.* Keep us in reality—not our esoteric fantasies of what is good for your people and what they need."

Esoteric, esoteric, Birú repeated to himself so he could look up the word as soon as possible and add it to his rapidly growing vocabulary. He was assigned to work in the Inter-American Conference of Ministers of Labor where he learned the concepts if not the practices of organizing workers to demand greater rights.

By the time he returned to the Viru valley and his sweetheart, he was changed so much that at first he had trouble making Marisa believe that he still wanted her to be his wife. No longer did he work in the fields but went to work with the Union as an organizer. Here is where he learned the politics of taking from one and giving to another. No man who believes that the labor of his workers is his property to be done with as he chooses welcomes a union organizer. Sometimes, the union movement was strong, when it had backing from the United States and European unions, and other times when the old aristocracy asserted itself there was nothing to do but lay quiet and not risk everything because in the end as long as the elites controlled the military, there was only so much you could do. Perhaps the most useful skill Birú had learned in the United States was not to be intimidated by those who lived in a world of entitlement, those who had been told from their birth that they had rights and expectations of service to them and their class by the members of the lower class. Birú had learned that these were good men and women who loved their children, who hurt and were hurt by the same forces of nature and life that he was. Because he understood them, like them, he was able to speak to them in their language, to make them understand that if their laborers earned more they would spend more and the economy would increase for everyone. Of course, there were those who would never listen and accused Birú and the labor movement of being communists intent on seizing their property and bringing the country to ruin.

Birú had not wanted to go into politics but knew that representing the voices of his people meant being there when important decisions were made. Now, at the culmination of his career, he had been elected governor of the province. "Jim should come to see what he helped start," Birú thought and instructed his secretary to send Jim one of the ornate hand-lettered invitations to his inauguration.

12

Jim lay in a hammock in the backyard of his home in one of the suburbs built around Washington in the post World War II boom, a boom that had never ended. Though he'd been living there for fifteen years after his divorce from Trish, he always felt as if he was living in someone else's house, as if the those who had built it, raised their family there had some permanent claim on the house. Maybe if he'd had the money to remodel or do more than the most necessary maintenance the old paint, appliances, and rugs would not have seemed so used and belonging to someone else.

There was a big division in his generation of those who had made money, lots of money, and those who had not. People like Zach had built their own homes, sold them and moved into bigger homes. People like him who were the remnants of the middle class lived like this, from paycheck to paycheck. Even though he was a pediatrician, he had to work extra hours to pay his alimony and the bills for his two sons' private school. Gone were the days of his father who took what jobs he wanted and moved his family around the world, always with enough money for whatever they needed.

Sunlight flittered through the green leaves of the old hickory tree above him, reflecting off the stiff paper of the invitation elaborately written in Spanish inviting him to Birú's inauguration.

On the invitation was a handwritten note—"Please speak to Zach. Tell him I would be honored if he came."

Jim smiled. Birú had changed in many ways. He knew how to manipulate people now. Zach had surely been sent his own invitation, but Birú knew that it would take Jim to actually get the great Zach Taylor to come to his event. Well, that was all right with Jim. If Zach wanted to go he would. Not Jim or anyone else he knew could talk Zach into doing something he did not want.

The nearly 40 years since he'd met Birú seemed to have gone by with the fool's illusion that life would last forever and there would always be time to do what he'd always meant to do. As he looked back, the dreams they'd had in South America seemed like childish fantasies incapable of withstanding the realities of life. Only Birú had lived to become what few could have imagined.

Jim's father had died soon after his hurried return from South America. After jobs including working at a food co-op in the roughest part of D.C., driving a taxi and delivering mail, he'd gone into the family business of medicine. Trish had gone with him when he went to Iowa to attend medical school. They'd been married soon after he started his residency at Georgetown.

Zach had not made his fortune in music but on Wall Street. Going with him would mean lux all the way. Zach might even fly them down on one of his jets. The problem was getting in touch with Zach. He used to keep a private cell phone for his close friends to reach him, but too many ex-lovers were on that list so now you had to go through his personal secretary.

Jim dialed the number and left the message. It was a couple of days before Zach called back, but Jim was in the middle of seeing patients, a constant stream with a set amount of time allotted for each child. He left another message and asked that Zach call back in the evening or on Sunday. Jim knew that was not likely, so figured he'd have to wait for the rare time when both were free and the urge to call had struck Zach.

* * *

"Why do you think Birú invited me?" Zach asked over the noise and vibration of the Gulfstream as they flew down to Peru. Jim and he were seated at a table in two comfortable airline chairs. In the back sat members of Zach's staff, satisfied-looking professionals whose attentive upright posture were a contrast to their boss' careless slouch.

Jim set his beer down next to the remnants of a delicious lunch of cold lobster salad. A very attractive employee of the company stepped from the front gallery to clear the plates.

"Do you mean besides all this?" Jim waved his hand vaguely toward the staff. "He is after all the newly-elected governor of Tumbes. I'm sure he's hoping for you to advise him on investments."

Zach's smile reminded Jim of his younger version.

"I was kind of hoping he wanted me there because of what I'd advised him about when he first came to the D.C.."

Jim laughed. "Now ZT, don't go ruining his inauguration with tales of debauchery."

"Attempted debauchery. He would only go so far, but I tried."

"That's probably the main reason he invited you. Why did you come?"

"Well, I...we have business down there."

"In Tumbes?" Jim asked.

Zach shook his head and frowned. "Of all the places in Latin America for us to be returning. At least this time we should be able to get out there when we want."

Jim laughed deeply, "I was just remembering you hopping over that counter, freaking out the clerk."

"Well he got us on the next bus. We might still be there." The somber, almost morose Zach returned. "Wish we could just take off, grab our packs, catch a bus and head out."

Jim matched his somber tone of voice. "Yeah, those days are gone."

One of his aides answered a buzzing phone.

"It's London," he half-shouted over the sound of the jet.

Zach shook his head. "Later," he said.

The aide relayed the message to whoever was on the phone in London and waited for the next service he could perform for Zach.

"It never ends. I can't take a shit without someone knowing about it. You know what it was?" Zach leaned forward the old light in his eyes. "It was freedom, pure freedom."

Jeffrey Marcus Oshins is a multi-instrumentalist who records and performs as Apokaful. He is the author of numerous novels and a travelogue.`

www.ingramcontent.com/pod-product-compliance
Lightning Source LLC
LaVergne TN
LVHW091341110826
845155LV00049B/24/J

* 9 7 9 8 9 8 7 7 8 8 7 2 1 *